TANSY
AND THE
2000
EARTH QUAKES

i

Dee Ann Bogue

TANSY
AND THE
2000
EARTH QUAKES

Dee Ann Bogue

Copyright © 2012 by Dee Ann Bogue.

ISBN: Softcover   978-1-4691-8179-0
           Ebook   978-1-4691-8180-6

All rights reserved. No part of this book may be reproduced or transmitted in any form or by any means, electronic or mechanical, including photocopying, recording, or by any information storage and retrieval system, without permission in writing from the copyright owner.

This is a work of fiction. Names, characters, places and incidents either are the product of the author's imagination or are used fictitiously, and any resemblance to any actual persons, living or dead, events, or locales is entirely coincidental.

This book was printed in the United States of America.

To order additional copies of this book, contact:
Xlibris Corporation
1-888-795-4274
www.Xlibris.com
Orders@Xlibris.com
100913

ACKNOWLEDGEMENTS

"Too much thank you" my German neighbor used to say. The following people deserve more than "too much thank you" for assistance, suggestions, editing, and sharing my fascination with the New Madrid earthquakes:

Julie Otrugman and the Creative Writing classes at Lincoln County Community College for more than ten years; my closest friends and confidants Dorothy Rogers and Karen Shafer; Dorothy's "No Name" book club who read an early draft and gave me strong but useful criticism; my son Eric who tramped around New Madrid with me checking out the museum, cemetery, and lay of the land; my son Todd who plans to market this book and make us both rich (!); my son Kipp who finally graduated from college this year in his 50s and is starting his own writing career; to Alana Ferrell and Ann Snodgrass for precision editing and correcting what I thought was already excellent; and especially to my talented and patient husband, Pete, who is dearly loved by me, and coincidently is an expert at the computer saving me from many technological meltdowns.

Dee Ann Bogue
Lincoln City, Oregon
March 1, 2012

REFERENCES

I found the following resources to be very helpful and engrossing. I spent hours reading about the earthquakes, increasing my passion for the subject day by day.

Barbara Brenner, *On the Frontier With Mr. Audubon* (Coward, McCann & Geoghegan, Inc., 1977).

James Lal Penick, Jr., *The New Madrid Earthquakes, Revised Edition*, (Columbia & London: University of Missouri Press, 1981).

Col. John Shaw, "New Madrid Earthquake Account of Col. John Shaw," *Missouri Historical Review*, (January 6, 1912).

Dr. David Stewart and Dr. Ray Knox, *The Earthquake America Forgot* (Marble Hill, MO: Gutenberg-Richter Publications, 1995).

Dr. David Stewart and Dr. Ray Knox, *The Earthquake That Never Went Away* (Marble Hill, MO: Gutenberg-Richter Publications, 1996).

* * *

CHAPTER 1

JULY 1811

I sat on the muddy riverbank, my two brothers' bodies lying cold and still beside me. In spite of the summer heat, I shivered uncontrollably, for I felt something leave me at that moment—something fine—maybe it was a kind of peace that had been true and real just hours before.

* * *

For days we had been heading down the Ohio River on a flatboat to live near Mama's sister in New Madrid, Missouri. The boys had been acting silly, running and pushing each other all around the deck. I'd had to settle them down time after time, but I couldn't settle Mama; she was just being that not-quite-right self she had become since last winter when Papa died.

I would never forget that day back in Pennsylvania. She had run outside crying, barefoot in the snow. Obadiah and Thomas and I, we called her to come back in the house where it was warm, but she stayed out in the barn all night. And ever after that, she would pay no mind to anything serious.

She had been no help when selling our sheep farm and packing up to move. Her mind was "touched" the neighbors said, and they told me I should take her out west to her sister's place. They thought we three needed an adult to care for us.

I had been sure I could handle our lives all right without our father, and with Mama being so different. After all, I, Tansy Grace Squires, was fourteen years old, and most times the boys would mind me. But as it turned out, I'd had more trouble than I expected with Mama.

Those thoughts had been running through my head as I watched my mother flounce around the deck, frolicking like our sheep used to do on a warm summer day back in Pennsylvania. She had twirled, hopped, and dipped, and everyone could see her ankles! I sat back stiffly with my arms folded, terribly embarrassed, but she didn't care. She'd even flirted with the crewmen, especially the red-haired one who played the harmonica. She laughed when their eyes met and then swished her skirt a little higher. Oh, Mama, how could you?

Seems like months ago we had boarded this flatboat in Pittsburgh. I could hardly wait to turn the boys over to Uncle Silas, for they needed a man's firm hand. Then maybe I could finally draw a breath of freedom. Aunt Mary had written us that there were plenty of bears and foxes to hunt, and wolves, panthers, and deer too. Uncle Silas would teach my brothers to shoot. My, how they were looking forward to that.

Whiling away the time on board, there hadn't been much else to do but slap mosquitoes and daydream. We would be there soon, I'd heard someone say. Just after we left the Ohio and turned into the Mississippi, it wouldn't be too much longer. We would pass by a few islands, go around a sharp bend, and there would be New Madrid!

The sun had been shining hard while we floated along, and it was plenty warm. Wetness under my arms had crept through my bodice and left damp stains on my frock. This had been happening more often lately and I was perplexed about this part of growing up. But the excitement of the travel thrust my thoughts outward. We waved at folks in the towns along the river. Once, I became a mite fearful when a canoe full of Indians paddled along side us. They only wanted whiskey and didn't seem ready to scalp us—at least not yet.

Mama had sat, finally, smoothing her silk dress and fanning herself. Whenever the music started up, she laughed and started dancing again, the ribbons of her straw bonnet fluttering out behind her. The boys had returned to their game of dominoes, arguing about whose turn it was. I went back to stitching my sampler, for I'd hoped to have it finished by the time we arrived at New Madrid. I'd planned to give it to Aunt Mary. She'd been so good to invite us to come and live near her. Of course she needed help with the baby, too, for she hadn't been well since Letty was born. I guess birthing a child is hard when you're getting old.

While I stitched, I had been thinking again about our new home. A tiny thrill of excitement pulsed through me. What would lie ahead, I wondered?

Captain Mickleson had plunked down on a barrel near us. "See over there, you young folks." He pointed to the north shore. "That's where them squirrels come a'runnin' right into this here Ohio River." He scratched his whiskers, making a rough sound. "Yes indeed, last time I come by here. By the hundreds, they come, and just run down and drowned theirselves dead as old fish.

We seen their bodies floatin' by. Belly up and bloated they was."

We had gasped at the picture he put in our minds of dead squirrels floating by.

"Now over there, yonder, is that there Cave-in-Rock." He nodded toward the cliffs. "See that yawnin' hole up ahead?"

We craned our necks to see, but it was hard to make out. Finally we found it by squinting our eyes.

"Used to be full o' bandits, sure enough was," he said. "Them'd come down and board the boats, then kill all the crew and haul their goods down to N'Orleans. Sell it fer handsome profits, they did. But Ol' Man Tuttle, he got kilt by one o' his own men. Served him right, the scoundre . . .

"Look alive, Lads!" he'd bellowed, jumping up. "We be leavin' the Ohio now," he said to the young folks.

The crew had scrambled to their posts. Three of them pushed the steering oar hard to the left as it slowly started turning the creaking craft into the big river. Many of us crowded up front, being mindful not to trip over the gear and cargo on deck. We were eager to see the great Mississippi. It wouldn't be long now before we reached New Madrid.

Just then, the boat slammed into something underwater. It jerked us all hard, popping the boat up on one side as it sank down on the other. Folks flew downhill on the tilted deck! Screams filled the air! Terrified, people fell into the river along with chickens, whiskey, barrels of sugar and molasses—even the fire in the big iron box where dinner had been cooking, went into the water!

"Mother!" I shrieked, clawing the air. But she and my brothers disappeared into the churning river, Mama still sitting on a barrel, going in backwards. My brothers' arms kept grasping for help that wasn't there. I fairly flew into the water myself, and landed hard on the edge of a floating box, tearing a gash in my cheek and ripping my sleeve. Chickens flapped and squawked all around me. Barrels banged into me. I grabbed one to keep afloat, frantically looking all around me for Mama and the boys. I tried to shout, but gasped and choked, swallowing so much water. The barrel slid out of my grasp! I thrashed my arms, trying to keep my head above the waves. My dress had wrapped around my legs, and I could hardly move them. I was terrified, and sinking! *I'm drowning! Drowning!*

More screams! Squawking! Voices calling for help! Gurgling! Bodies disappearing! Flapping wings brushed my face. Splashing water blurred the scene before me.

Deck hands tried salvaging supplies, their arms scrabbling for flotsam while it kept toppling into the river. Why weren't they saving us? Was the freight more important than people?

"Grab them cages there, men! Push 'em back up on the deck!" a loud voice hollered.

Another shouted, "I got 'em, Cap'n. But I can't crawl up a hill, damn it! The boat's still tiltin'!"

"Mama!" I screamed. "Obadiah! Thomas!" I couldn't see any of them. Just boxes, other people, bodies grabbing, clinging together!

Mama's bonnet floated past me. I grabbed for it, but it was empty.

I don't remember much else, except waking up on this muddy shore. Other people were there, all soaking wet, some sobbing, some lying still. The red-headed boatman stood knee-deep in the river pulling on an arm, dragging it toward shore. It was my little brother.

"Obadiah!" I screamed. "Come here. Where is Mama? And Thomas?" The red-head dragged the limp body out of the water and lay him beside me. Only then, with a shock that stung like lightning, did I understand. My brother was dead.

"Obadiah! No! No! My brother! My little brother!" I lay myself across his wet body, clinging hard, and rocked him back and forth, sobbing helplessly.

"Is this your brother, too, Miss?" I rolled over and looked up. The red-head held Thomas draped over his arms like a wet blanket. I could see he was also dead.

"Oh no. Not Thomas, too." My sobs became a wail. Loud wails that wrenched my whole body. I pounded the sandy shore over and over with my fists, whether rage or fear, I knew not.

That's the moment when that something left me. Was it peace? Or life itself? Certainly all the dreams and excitement for a new life vanished. In their place an eerie, heavy stoniness settled deep within me.

My voice sounded flat when I said, "Give him to me, Sir. I will take care of him. And please, Sir, my mother? Do you know where she is?" I asked him. But I knew she was gone too.

"Ain't seen her, Miss. "Howsomever, I'm bringin' in the bodies that keeps comin'." He waded back into the water, grasped a carpet bag with one hand and steered a floating box toward shore with the other.

Wailing and moaning continued, filling the air, along with shouts of survivors and crew. I heard myself wailing, too, as I pushed the boys' hair off their faces and straightened out their arms and legs.

I sat on that muddy shore long past sundown, not far from New Madrid, Missouri. I sat there with my two dead brothers beside me, and the loss of my mother rock-heavy on my heart. I felt all trembly inside, like leaves on a willow tree. Why? Where? What now?

I stopped trembling suddenly, for some people came toward me. They insisted I come to their cabin to dry off and have some supper. I tried to refuse, for I didn't want to leave my brothers. But Captain Mickelson was there and said his men were gathering the bodies, and there would be a funeral the next day. He told me to go with the kind folks, and no, my mother's body had not been found, but they were still looking.

"We'll hitch some horses to the flatboat and right it in the morning, Miss. Then, after a service for the departed, we'll be on our way." The captain spoke gently.

I couldn't bear his words. "Oh, please, Sir," I cried, getting up on my knees. "Please don't make us go! I can't leave without my mother! She . . ." I grasped his hand with both of mine.

"Some bodies we'll never find, Miss." He shook me off and walked away, barking orders to the crew.

Tears burst again from my eyes like a rainstorm, and great wails I couldn't halt gushed forth.

The funeral service next day was pitiful. Six bodies had been recovered, my brothers' being the smallest. Folks gathered in a clearing beyond some cabins where a large hole had been dug. Captain Mickelson read a Psalm and said a prayer, and then those who weren't crying sang *My Faith Looks Up to Thee*. I could not join in song for my crying, but softened it so as not to disturb others. The heaviness within me grew into a throbbing ache.

* * *

CHAPTER 2

THE NEXT DAY

"All aboard!" Captain Mickelson's words pierced the silence surrounding the dazed passengers waiting on shore.

The flatboat had been righted and repaired. The crew, urged by the captain to hurry, loaded the salvaged gear on deck and hauled up anchor.

I boarded with the others, still wearing my gingham dress. It had finally dried, but was ragged and muddy. Mama's carpetbag had been salvaged. In it I found the green silky dress she so loved, a shift, stockings, and lacy drawers, and a fancy feather bonnet, now crushed. Everything was soggy and smelled of the river. I could never bring myself to wear any of those. For one thing, they were far too small. I was nearly a head taller than Mama. She was so tiny. "No bigger than a minute," Papa used to say.

The crew poled the boat out into the current of the fast-flowing Mississippi River. They busily kept us on course dodging floating snags here and there. The river was browner now, and flowed faster than the Ohio. Thick cypress forests grew along the banks, and we passed small islands covered with trees. Oak and cottonwood, the captain said.

This land looked nothing like the gentle hills and pastures of Pennsylvania. I would miss the bleating of sheep and the wildflowers along the fences, especially the nodding heads of yellow tansy ragwort. Mama named me after them, she had said, because I was dainty like they were. She didn't know then I would grow so tall. Everything here seemed foreign to me, and facing it without Mama and the boys gave a bitter sickness to my stomach and caused tears to flow.

Tiny no-see-ums swarmed around my head and in my nose and eyes. They were such an annoyance! They made me far angrier than I remember ever being before. I slapped and fussed at them, only delaying their onslaught, for they came back in charge after charge. I pulled my bonnet close about my head and face so that only my eyes could see out. I didn't want to miss New Madrid as we approached it. The captain said that when we rounded a curve in the river and headed north, it would come into view. Then around another curve, there it would be.

And so it was. Before I knew it, the boat had pulled into a small inlet. The red-headed crewman—his name was Bart, I had learned—shoved a pole into the shallow water and pushed us forward until I heard the bottom scrape, and we stopped with a jerk.

A few people stood on shore. I spotted a tall thin woman carrying a baby, and I knew it must be Aunt Mary. Behind her, holding the harness of a mule, was a man with a full gray beard wearing a tattered straw hat. I wondered if that could be Uncle Silas.

Carrying my mother's carpetbag and another bundle of salvaged items, I followed two other passengers down the gangplank. I realized Aunt Mary would be looking for Mama and three children. It would be up to me to tell her the dreadful news.

"Aunt Mary?" I asked, approaching the tall woman with graying hair pulled into a knot on top of her head. "I am Tansy Grace Squires, your niece from Pennsylvania."

This woman nodded her head and looked down at me, not saying a word. Then she lifted her eyes and looked beyond me. I knew she was searching for her sister, my mother.

"Aunt Mary," I tried again. "There was a terrible accident." I hated to go on, but knew I must. Tears flooded my eyes making them blurry, and my words tumbled out in no special order.

"Mama drowned. The boys are buried." Trying to make clear what happened, I stuttered, "The f-f-flatboat tipped and . . ."

Aunt Mary's face drained of color. The mule behind her made an awful noise and shifted its feet, stepping on the man I was sure was Uncle Silas.

"Git off my lame foot, you dad-burned mule!" he yelled, shoving the animal against Aunt Mary.

She lost her footing and fell forward into me, baby and all. I dropped the carpet bag and caught the baby while Aunt Mary righted herself.

"Glory be! Tansy! My niece? Oh dear, Letty! Are you hurt, child?" Aunt Mary took the baby from me. "Pearly, you say? You say my sister Pearly drowned?"

I do not remember the rest of that day. Somehow I ended up here, in Aunt Mary and Uncle Silas's house, in this small bed in a large room. I must have had some supper since I was not at all hungry. I knew I must have told Aunt Mary more about the dreadful happenings on the river, for my eyes were swollen from crying. I was so tired, so lonely, so heartsick. I would try to sleep. Maybe tomorrow I could think clearly and sort things out.

* * *

CHAPTER 3

OCTOBER 1811

I had hoped life in New Madrid would be much different from our farm life in Pennsylvania. The river, of course, and the people weren't the same. But back there I'd had to see about things since Mama had been little help. I'd barely known how to sell the place or pack for our trip. And I'd had a hard time making sure the boys were clean and sensible. They were often contrary about obeying me. "You're not my mother," one or the other would shout. "I don't have to obey you!" After they were in bed, I'd sometimes end the day crying my eyes out.

I had been so relieved when that letter from Aunt Mary arrived asking us to come to New Madrid. Now, after four months, it seemed like I would still be in charge. I had hoped to fit into the background of this family somehow, and just be a girl. But here I was, making decisions again, and I just didn't know how to do it very well. Especially decisions about a baby and poor Aunt Mary who had something she called "floating-away" spells.

Well, I was in this family now, stumbling along trying to find my place. But some things were so frustrating and caused me no little amount of grief. Mostly Uncle Silas, who, although he was shorter than I, filled the room with his presence whenever he was in it. It was his house after all, and I knew I must respect him. But he seemed strange. I just wasn't sure what to think about him. Twice now, he's stood so close to me, I could feel his warm tobacco breath on my neck. Once, his boot slid under my skirt and leaned against my foot. It made me feel crowded somehow, and when I backed up, I tripped and fell into the wood box. When I grabbed for something to break my fall, Uncle Silas took my hand and pulled me up, but he didn't let go until I wrenched myself free. His hand felt rough and stiff and hot, and a shudder rippled through me. I hurried into the back room to see about Aunt Mary.

Later, I ducked under the low doorframe and stepped outside into the fall sunlight. It was time to feed the roosters again. Uncle Silas wanted them strong and healthy for the next cockfight, so I must not be slothful, but I dearly dreaded that chore. He had bred his roosters to be good fighters. And they were. They flew at me, pecking me until I could dash out of the gate. How I detested them, but crossing Uncle Silas would be—well, never mind, Tansy.

I dragged myself along, day after day, helping Aunt Mary with the baby and the house and the roosters. Pictures of that terrible time last summer so often flashed into my mind. The commotion, the screams, the flapping chickens and thrashing water, and me, trying to hang onto a floating barrel. I kept remembering the gasping and choking, and being so fearful of drowning, and all the while I was still clutching my silly sampler I'd been stitching on the flatboat!

And I wondered where Mama's body was. I fretted about her every day. She had been such a part of me. I felt as if I'd lost a leg or an arm. My throat tightened just thinking about her, like when I was a little girl and was scolded for spilling cider. Or when Obadiah or Thomas teased me. Oh my poor brothers! Thoughts of them today made me sob as hard as when their bodies were put into the ground and covered with dirt.

I forced the pictures of the past out of my mind and dashed out of the chicken yard. Uncle Silas's roosters were all fed now, pecking away at the grain. I hurried back inside the house and picked up Letty from the puncheon floor. I hoped she wouldn't get more slivers from its rough wood, for then she would cry so.

Time I changed her again and then pumped some water before starting dinner. I laid Letty on my bed in the big room. She grabbed my bonnet strings, pulling the bow undone.

"No no, pretty maid," I said, retying it. She giggled and rolled her hips over so that I had a hard time wrapping the infant towel around her.

"Hold still, Letty. Let me tie your bonnet too, and we'll go outside and see if Mr. Joe is there."

Letty clapped her hands with glee. I picked her up and realized how much she had grown in four months.

"I say, child, you're getting mighty heavy for your cousin to carry. Seems to me you're a very big girl for nearly nine months old."

Outside, I sat Letty down against a log and scanned the treetops for Mr. Joe. He came swooping down and landed on the woodpile, his black feathers glinting with greens and blues.

"There you are, you ol' beggar crow. Just waiting for us to bring you some scraps, I suppose?"

I pulled some dried corn kernels out of my pocket and tossed them near the chopping block. Mr. Joe cawed loudly, fluffed his wing feathers and tipped his head back.

Then he hopped to the ground and pecked at the kernels, keeping a safe distance from us. Mrs. Joe watched from up in the persimmon tree. She never ventured down when we were outside. She must be guarding Mr. Joe, I guessed.

The pump creaked as water splashed into the bucket. Letty started crawling toward Mr. Joe, but I scooped her up into my arms. "Oh Letty girl," I told her as I brushed dirt off her hands and plain brown dress. "You'll have to learn to walk soon. Then you can come out here without getting so dirty."

As I started back into the house, Letty in one arm and the bucket of water in the other, she reached toward Mr. Joe crying with loud screams and gulps, arms and legs thrashing.

"Better walk before snow time gets here," I told her, "when we can hardly get outside at all."

Aunt Mary had told me this coming winter would be another hard one just like last year. Then she'd sighed at the thought. She'd said more than once the 1810 winter was the worst she and Uncle Silas had endured since moving here eleven years ago. Seemed like she sighed quite often lately. For a week, now, she's been a mite bilious, she'd told me. I didn't rightly know about that, but she didn't seem very well.

I shuddered just thinking about snow. It always put me in mind of that day way back in Pennsylvania when Papa died.

Oh pshaw! There I go again. I tied my apron on over my green gingham dress, rolled up my sleeves, and steered my thoughts back to supper. Uncle Silas would be in from the field 'soon, and Aunt Mary would need more of her medicine.

Why did I start thinking about Papa and Mama again? I tried so hard not to, but horrid pictures of those days just slipped back into my mind. Over and over. The only time I didn't think about losing my family was when I was caring for Letty, or we were watching Mr. Joe. Letty would light up so, with smiles and giggles. Then a warmth would flow through me like I'd never known before. I felt such a pleasing attachment to the child that I didn't understand, but I declare was dearly welcome.

She played with her tin cup on the floor while I put water on to boil for cornmeal mush. Aunt Mary seemed to tolerate that right well. I sighed again and snapped my attention back to today just as Letty grabbed a candle off the windowsill and stuffed it into her mouth.

"No, Letty. No! You can't eat the candle!" Dashing to her, I ran my finger around inside her lips, pulling out bits of wax and black wick.

"Shame, little girl!" I put a hard biscuit in her cup. Letty shook it out and began sucking on it, then crawled to the door and started over the sill to go outside.

"No again, Letty!" Grabbing her by one leg, I dragged her inside and sat down on the floor, pulling her onto my lap. Turning her around, I pressed her warm body against mine and held her tightly, rocking back and forth, giving myself over to her warm softness, while she squirmed to get down.

"Oh come now, give Cousin Tansy a hug." She hugged me back, wriggling pleasure deep into my heart.

Outside, Mr. Joe was watching us, his head cocked to one side. "Wave to Mr. Joe, Letty," I told her, waving her hand with mine. I stepped outside with her and started singing the ditty she loved:

One crow anger, two crows, mirth.
Three crows a wedding, four crows a birth.
Five crows heaven, six crows hell,
But seven is the devil's own self.

I began to sing it again, *One crow anger, two crows . . .* but stopped when I heard the uneven scrunch of Uncle Silas's boots. He rounded the corner of the house, limping from his old arrow wound, and holding onto the wall to steady himself. My shoulders tensed whenever he came home, for his piercing eyes would examine me from head to toe for some time before speaking, making me feel—exposed.

"Git that danged crow outa' this yard." He limped toward the chopping block and picked up the ax. As he passed close to me I could smell Uncle Silas's tobacco and sweat mixed with alcohol.

"I'm telling you for the last time, girl, them danged critters eatin' every bit of corn they can hold." He hoisted the ax over his head and aimed it at Mr. Joe, who flitted safely away up to a tree limb.

"I'll put 'em in the stewpot if they keep comin' around." Uncle Silas sent the ax onto a round of wood, caught it, and lobbed it up onto the chopping block.

"And git that baby inside. It be gittin' dark soon." He cleared his throat noisily and spat off toward the woodpile.

"Don't want that baby breathin' the night air, all full of poison an' such, doncha know. Git sick like her ma." He stacked the split pieces of wood onto a pile. "Don't need no more sick females here." He turned around and began chopping again, muttering to himself about bad night air and spirits causing sickness.

One crow anger . . . I recited to myself. I wished Uncle Silas wouldn't carry on so about his superstitions. Standing up with Letty in my arms, I went back into the house. But I ducked my head too late and bumped it on the splintery lintel. My bonnet scraped off, and several of my dark brown hairs caught and were left hanging.

"Oh, that hurts!" I cried, rubbing my head.

"Ooh," Letty cooed, watching my reaction.

Just then I heard Aunt Mary's weak voice calling from the back room. "Tansy, oh Tansy."

Oh dear! I was late with her medicine. She should have had it an hour ago. Quickly knotting my hair and retying my bonnet, I hurried inside. I grabbed the laudanum on my way and pushed open the back room door.

Aunt Mary seemed so pale lying on the bed, her face almost gray like her wispy hair. Even under the quilt her long frame seemed thinner today. Looking at Aunt Mary was a shock. Of course she was quite old—almost forty-two.

"Here's your medicine, Aunt Mary. You've been sleeping so long; I didn't want to wake you." I put cheer in my voice that I didn't feel.

"I wish you'd begin to get better," I added. I counted out twenty drops of laudanum and dripped them on her tongue. She made a face at the bitter taste, and sank back on the pillow. After a few moments, she roused some.

"Bring me my mirror, Tansy," she said weakly. "It's in the trunk over yonder."

I had wondered what might be in that trunk. Opening the heavy lid, I found the round mirror, its frame and handle of smooth, rosy wood. It sat atop some pale, blue fabric that caught the fading light from the window in its rich folds. Letty came crawling into her mother's room, squealing all the way. She pulled herself up to the edge of the high bed. The straw mattress crinkled softly as Aunt Mary moved over. I boosted Letty up next to her mother.

"Now hand me that velvet redingote, girl. And that fancy comb." Her voice seemed stronger now as she reached out and took the mirror and the soft blue velvet coat.

"See here, Letty? Will you wear fancy clothes like this when you are a fine young lady?" She caressed Letty's cheek with the soft cloth. Letty giggled and blinked, shaking her head this way and that, her blonde curls peeking out from under her bonnet, bouncing merrily. She crawled to the foot of the bed, babbling pleasant baby sounds.

"Maybe you'll go to a fine dance and meet the president like I did, child." Aunt Mary lay back on the pillow and closed her eyes. "And you'll go to school in Paris, ma Cherie, and learn to play the pianoforte and sing and paint, and . . ."

"It's time to get dinner ready, Tansy. Uncle Silas will be hungry after shocking all that corn today." Aunt Mary dismissed me with the same soft voice she used for Letty. She had told me about many things from her past and going to all those places when she lived in Paris. Now she wants them for Letty. I could tell she was feeling a little better just talking about them. I hoped she would be up and around tomorrow.

"Shall I leave Letty with you, Aunt Mary?" It was quite a job, taking care of this baby while seeing to the cooking and other necessities. Letty was into everything lately: the wood box, the flour bin, especially the barrel of sugar. And oh, the messes she made that I had to clean up!

"Yes, she can stay here for now." Aunt Mary propped herself up and gazed into the mirror. As I left the room, I caught a glimpse of her holding the redingote under her chin with one hand, and she was combing her wispy hair down flat from its center part with the other. But wait! Did I really see what I thought I saw as I left the room? Was Aunt Mary smiling at herself in the mirror?

* * *

CHAPTER 4

NOVEMBER 1811

Today was mighty warm for November, I thought. I dipped water into the large pot hanging in the fireplace and swung it over the flames. I was glad it wasn't snowing yet, like last winter in Pennsylvania. Probably it would snow any day now. Be hard going then.

I added some sticks to the fire and stirred it to get a blaze going. Nights were cooling off considerably, but days were right pleasant. I sometimes started to tell Mama about the colored leaves, Mr. Joe, the murmur of the river. Then I'd remember—she was gone. Why couldn't I get it in my head once and for all?

Looking out the window, I sighed, thinking about what might have been. The persimmon tree had lost most of its leaves and looked forlorn against the gray sky. I hadn't seen Mr. or Mrs. Joe for a while.

I had been so eager for our family to live here in New Madrid. The boys would go to school and go hunting in the woods. I'd known they would grow up just fine here. And Mama would be content. Aunt Mary had wanted Mama to help her, since she was getting on past forty and had a new baby. Even though Mama wasn't quite right anymore, she could work hard. And oh how she loved to dance and sing! She thought she was coming here just to play with Baby Letty. And now it was only me left, and in another family.

I ground up a few roasted, blackened potatoes to make some coffee, even though I didn't like it much. I sure enough hoped that keelboat full of supplies would come soon so we'd get some real coffee. The water finally boiled, sending steam curling upward to the low ceiling and along the log beams supporting the loft. I dipped water into the pot and tossed in a handful of ground potatoes.

"Whar's supper?" Uncle Silas bellowed, limping into the room, tracking mud from his shoes.

"It's coming, Uncle Silas," I told him. "Just as soon as I stir this cornmeal a mite more, there'll be porridge. Ouch!" The bubbling porridge popped up, splattering my hand. I blew on it, then shook it hard.

"Whar's that baby now? I brought her a cricket to play with. Bring her some good luck. Heaven knows she needs some."

"She's in with Aunt Mary, Sir. Aunt Mary seems to be feeling better."

He pushed open the back room door and bounded across the floor, grabbing Letty roughly. He limped back out and sat down with her on his lap.

"What in thunder you doing, Miz Cummings?" he shouted to Aunt Mary. "Lettin' that baby look in a mirror? Bring that dinner here, Tansy. And you watch the child better, you understand?" He set Letty down, placing the cricket on her knee with care. It jumped onto her sleeve, and she squealed with pleasure, but fear, too, I perceived.

"Now feed her some of that mush before Miz Cummings nurses her. Got to keep Letty well. She might could die from lookin' in a mirror, don'cha know." He shook his head and cleared his throat loudly. "Thunderation!" he grumbled. "Folks mighty careless of a baby around here. Might be she needs a rabbit's foot, too."

That night, after darkness had covered the town, the pots all scrubbed and hung up, and the fire dwindling to coals, I sat in the maple rocker and picked up my sampler. I could hear Uncle Silas snoring in the back room. I sure enough hoped Aunt Mary could sleep through that noise. I tried not to think unpleasant thoughts about my uncle, but I declare he did have some peculiar beliefs and irritating ways.

At times Uncle Silas sent me out to the shed to gather eggs and then he followed me, and just stood there looking at me with his red, watery eyes. I didn't know what to say or do. I would feel all awkward and gangly. Once, when he came up close to me, I dropped an egg, and it broke. Then he scolded me harshly and said I was bewitching his house.

"Why'd you come here, girl?" he asked then, as he had at other times.

Sometimes he went off on his superstitions, and I would get all flustered and unsure of what was true and who I was, and why I was here. I found myself wondering all sorts of things, like why Aunt Mary married him and moved way out west. Life with Uncle Silas must have been some different for her than when she was married to Uncle Pierre. If I ever married, I'd live in Pennsylvania in a fine house. My husband would be handsome and maybe a banker, or I hoped at least not a farmer. But that was far away. No need to think about that. I was here now. My future was just that. Future.

I filled my mind with thoughts of sweet Letty with her bright blue eyes and constant curiosity. Another love feeling crept through my heart for that baby girl, something I hadn't ever felt before. Nothing else gave me peace these days. Especially when I thought about Aunt Mary. It was so worrisome since she'd been ailing. I felt grateful she had taken me in, but that was not the same as what I felt for Letty. 'Course Letty was into everything and got so dirty and all.

I had to get to bed, for I had early chores the next day. However, I decided I'd work on my sampler for a while first. I had started this back in Pennsylvania, but hadn't worked on it much here. This one looked better than the first one I embroidered when I was seven or eight. It gave me much pleasure then, but it seemed such a chore these days.

Each letter, in yellow silk thread, was a little better than the one before it. When the numbers were finished, I'd start on the verse in black silk. Mama had written it on the linen for me in brown ink, but it had faded some from being in the river, I guess. I'd better get busy, for the words were getting hard to read. *Tender-hearted, for—ing one another.* I could hardly make out some letters; I wasn't sure just what that said. Maybe *forsaking one another?* That didn't sound right, but I didn't know. Maybe *forgetting one another?* That was strange, too, but maybe there was some truth in it. I wondered . . .

Rocking quietly and drawing the needle in and out, I hummed a sad tune. I thought about how Aunt Mary never has gotten completely well. She had been shaking hard and either feverish or chilled for a week now, but today not so much. When she had smiled at herself in the mirror, what was she thinking about? Maybe about when she lived in Pennsylvania or way back in France, when she wore the blue velvet redingote. It was so pretty and soft. She was Madame Pierre Chartier then. Mama always said, "My sister Mary married well and went to high-falutin' parties. She even met President Jefferson once." I thought Mama wished she had married well, too. Papa was "just a plain farmer" Mama used to say.

But both sisters' husbands had died, and now Aunt Mary was the wife of Uncle Silas, although I couldn't fathom why. He was so different from Uncle Pierre, who always made me laugh. I wished Uncle Silas wasn't so cranky and superstitious. He was a farmer, too, like Papa, but mostly he raised roosters for cock fights. I didn't think Aunt Mary was pleased about that. She drew her mouth together like a draw-string purse when he loaded the roosters into the wagon and left home for a day or two. The air seemed stiff as a bristle brush those times. Didn't seem like there was much peace between times, either. Maybe I'd never ever marry, for I wanted to live in peace more than anything in this world. There now. I bit off the thread, for the alphabet was all finished and right pretty, I thought.

My thoughts had rambled, but stopped suddenly, like running into a tree. I didn't want to think about Uncle Silas anymore, or his smell or his spitting, or how peculiar I felt when he came close to me. The creak of the rocker woke Letty, who coughed and whined, then all was silent again. Only the sound of a brisk night breeze blowing through the trees could I faintly hear.

I forced my thoughts to the next day. I'd had a longing to walk down to the river lately, before the cold winter came, and the snow kept us confined inside the house. I closed my eyes and sang a favorite song of mine.

It's Cindy in the springtime,
It's Cindy in the fall.
If I can't have my Cindy gal,
I'll have no gal at all.

Singing was always so pleasant with Mama, but now a tightness pinched my insides every time I thought of her and the boys. Well, it was getting late. I got up and stirred the fire, covered Letty and made sure the door was bolted tightly against the night air. Maybe the night air was tying my insides in a knot. Uncle Silas would say so. I crawled into bed and hummed myself to sleep to the rhythm of Letty's soft breathing and the soft night wind.

Aunt Mary cried out, waking me from a sound sleep. Was it early morning, or the middle of the night? It was still dark and cold. I quickly got up, lit the lamp, and rushed into her room. Oh dear. She was shaking and coughing so! Yesterday, she was feeling better, but now how bad she sounded! And where was Uncle Silas? It must be morning, and he would be out in the barn.

I gave Aunt Mary twenty drops of laudanum with a spoonful of whiskey. Maybe that would help her. Uncle Silas had been telling me it would. I stirred the coals in the fireplace, adding some wood to get the fire going and cooked up a batch of porridge. When I brought it to Aunt Mary, she thanked me and smiled weakly, but wouldn't eat. What a worry this sickness was!

After a little while, though, she had calmed a bit. "You must get away this afternoon, Tansy, and take a walk." Aunt Mary spoke slowly and with some effort. I could barely hear her.

"Thank you kindly, Aunt Mary. It is good of you to think of me, when you are so sick. I'll go only if you are feeling well, and while Letty is sleeping." I was glad to see she had stopped shaking. I would be pleased to have a peaceful hour to myself.

I wanted to crawl back into my bed for a few more minutes of warmth, but it was time to cook up more porridge. Uncle Silas would be cantankerous if his meal wasn't hot when he returned from feeding the stock. I swung the heavy kettle over the flames, and then stood up, lingering by the fire to warm myself. Just then Uncle Silas clomped inside. Staring hard at me, he limped across the room and pulled me roughly against his stiff, cold coat.

"Hmm? You warm up your Uncle Silas, girl? Hmm?" His beard bristled into my neck, and he smelled of manure and tobacco. He held me close, rubbing his hands up and down my back. I recoiled at his advances, struggling to free myself, but he grasped me tighter, pressing my breasts against him until they hurt. In my twisting to back away, I knocked his hat off onto the floor. He let go of me suddenly, and stooped to retrieve it.

I was so repulsed, I fled outside. What could he mean? Had I encouraged him some way? Should I be expected to warm him? Was I being selfish? I shivered and shook for several minutes.

After a while I became chilled from the cold and thought perhaps I had dreamed this whole encounter. Inside, Uncle Silas was seated at the table, calmly eating a dish of porridge. Letty was waking, and I attended to her needs as usual.

Later, when Letty was napping, I wrapped my shawl around my shoulders, stepped outside, and breathed in the fall air. I could smell the river from here, and its tangy odor called to me. Seemed like I was drawn to the Mississippi maybe just like the squirrels that rushed into the Ohio. Of course, I wouldn't jump in the river and drown like thousands of them did! I've heard tell it was the comet that appeared earlier this year that drove them to do such an uncommon thing.

There had been terrible floods last spring, Aunt Mary said—the worst anyone ever heard of. And just a bit later was when Mama and the boys drowned. Oh, I mustn't start thinking that again! But this was a mysterious year, and I didn't like Missouri much. Would I ever feel at home here? I did think about leaving sometimes, but how? Or when? Where would I go?

Hurrying through town, I decided to climb the hill and go through the woods where I could see far up the river from the top of the cliff. I had a strong desire to see around the New Madrid bend and count the boats turning into the St. John's Bayou. Lots of folks got off there at the harbor and settled right here in New Madrid. And more came all the time. Would they all be content here, I wondered? Somehow I couldn't help but look for Mama and the boys when the passengers walked down that gangplank. 'Course that's foolishness I knew. They were swept away down the river. "They're gone, Tansy," I told myself. "All gone."

I walked faster through the trees and up the rise. From here I could see where St. John's Bayou flowed into the Mississippi. I was a mite out of breath, so I leaned against a walnut tree and looked through the woods out over the harbor. There must have been a hundred boats tied up or anchored there. Over yonder I saw four, no five more coming round the bend. I guessed they'd be stopping to leave passengers and stay the night, then be off by daybreak. In a few days they'd be in New Orleans. I wondered what that city was like. I'd heard tales about it being such an old city and full of exciting music, food, and people of all kinds and colors.

The graveyard was just across the bayou. That fresh dirt there, along the bluffs, must be Miz Southward's grave. She died last month of the consumption, Aunt Mary had said it was. Uncle Silas thought she probably had a bath this late in the season, and that did her in. I wondered if her ghost was coming out of . . . oh I don't believe that, but Uncle Silas said so.

What was that noise? Something like footsteps startled me. Maybe I felt something more than heard it. I didn't see anyone, but I got a peculiar feeling I was not alone. Behind a tree a shadow moved. A twig snapped. My breath stopped; my heart pounded like thunder. I tried to swallow, but couldn't. My throat made a little noise; and then, from behind that tree, I heard that same noise. I coughed. Strange, I heard the same kind of cough.

"Who's there?" I asked, my voice shaking.

"Who's there?" repeated a high-pitched voice.

"Who are you?"

"Who are you?" Again my same words. I strained to see through the brush and glimpsed a dark brown elbow, not much bigger than mine, sticking out from behind a tree.

"What do you want? Are you a runaway?" Everyone knew there were runaway slaves all over. Uncle Silas had said to watch out for them.

" . . . you a runaway?" The voice repeated and then added, "Free. Solomon free."

I felt less afraid at that. The word "free" had a lifting feel to it. I walked toward the voice. "Are you Solomon?" I asked cautiously.

A small brown man (or was he a boy?) stepped out from behind the tree. He was smiling a big smile, but something was strange about him. His face was caked with dirt, and drool was running down his chin. His eyes were wide open circles. I couldn't be sure, but they seemed, well, empty some way. He wore a strange turban with grey fur on the top.

"Eat?" he said. "You eat with Solomon?" He reached atop his turban and grabbed the fur thing, holding it out toward me. Oh! I couldn't believe what I saw. It was a rat! Its feet stuck up in the air, its long tail hanging straight down!

* * *

CHAPTER 5

EARLY DECEMBER 1811

I shrieked and backed up. Cold shivers crawled up my neck. My knees weakened, and I grabbed hold of a tree. I didn't like rats! Sometimes at night I heard them in the loft, and pulled the quilt over my head, shivering with dread.

Solomon came toward me, still offering the rat in outstretched hands. Something about this boy/man seemed harmless, yet the horror of this rat coming at me gave my mind a dizzy mix-up.

"Don't come near me," I called, my voice quivering. I held up my hand for him to stop.

"Don't come near me," he repeated in a sing-song voice. "Solomon not bad. Solomon give food. Eat." He held out the rat again and grinned.

"Drop that!" I pointed a shaky finger at him. "I don't want it."

Solomon sat on the ground, cross-legged, a pathetic, disappointed look on his light brown face.

"You no eat? Solomon good boy. See?" He put the rat back on his head, and wrapped his turban around it. Only the tail hung down over one ear.

I took a closer look at this shoeless person. He appeared to be about fifteen or maybe older, a light Negro, about as tall as I was, and very dirty. His ragged breeches and homespun shirt were not nearly warm enough for December. My eyes roamed over this strange-looking fellow while he looked plaintively back at me.

"Solomon good boy," he repeated. He opened his hands and looked down at them. "Want more food?"

I couldn't tell if that last was a question to me, or if he truly needed food, but I felt a tug of sympathy for him. I could almost hear Uncle Silas telling me to run away quickly, but I moved carefully toward Solomon and sat down beside him, still keeping a wary eye on him.

"Are you hungry, Solomon?" I asked. "Do you need food?" I glanced at his turban, cringing again at its contents. Would he truly eat rat? I knew some people did eat varmints; Uncle Silas said he did when he lived in Kentucky. But who was this person before me?

I stared at him. He smiled vacantly at me. Many things raced through my mind, while a chill wind blew through the trees, tossing a few stray leaves in the air. I knew I must get back home, but what to do right now?

"I must go," I told Solomon and stood up. "You—you go to the crewmen on the boats. They will give you food. See?" I pointed toward the harbor. "Go!" Suddenly I wanted no further conversation. I certainly didn't want him to follow me. I turned and ran toward home.

As I hurried from the forest, I spied colored persimmons on the ground, some partly covered by fallen leaves. Aunt Mary had said they were good to eat after the first frost, so I filled my apron with several. I would make persimmon pudding for supper, her favorite treat in winter, she had said.

Passing the Southwards' small brick house, I wondered how her family was getting on. Since I didn't see any smoke from their chimney, I assumed the boys were still in the fields with their pa. Sad loss for that family. Aunt Mary would want to take them some fixings if she were well. Maybe I could take them some pudding, if I had collected enough persimmons. Aunt Mary would be pleased, I was sure. She couldn't help lay out Miz Southward's body, and she felt mighty bad about that.

I walked faster, pulling my shawl closer about my shoulders. Maybe it would freeze tonight. I searched the sky for snow clouds, but it was clear. As twilight fell, the Great Comet appeared, with its two tails strung out behind like a kite. Such a strange thing, that comet. It didn't show up in the daytime. Oh dear, it must be later than I thought. I quickened my steps, but it was getting hard to see, and I nearly tripped a time or two on the uneven ground.

Passing the pig sty, I heard Uncle Silas talking with Mister Southward about the comet. They both knew what the Indians believed about it. To them it meant earthquakes were coming. Oh, I hoped not. I'd be so afraid! They mentioned Tecumseh's brother, that he had foretold an earthquake. He had prophesied last fall that the sun would disappear, and it did, for a time.

"We'd best be makin' star wishes ever' night, I'm thinking," she heard Uncle Silas say.

What a year this had been in Missouri! I just didn't like it here.

Darkness deepened as I came up the path to the house. I made out the faraway call of those wild passenger pigeons. So many more this year than last, Aunt Mary had said. Sometimes thousands at one time would darken the sky. They ate more corn than the crows, and that made Uncle Silas angry. Maybe he'd shoot some for tomorrow's dinner.

I thought about the beautiful Carolina parrots that I had seen lately. Their green feathered bodies and red and yellow heads brightened the dark forest. I was glad they didn't eat corn, for Uncle Silas would surely shoot them. Letty laughed and clapped her hands whenever she saw them. Bless that child. She didn't worry about causing her pa grief, but I did.

Oh pshaw! I could see he was almost finished feeding the pigs and all his roosters. He'd be wanting supper soon. *Hurry along, Tansy, hurry!*

In the house, all was quiet. That was good and it was bad. At least Letty was still sleeping, but when she napped a long time, she would stay awake late into the night. *I should have come home sooner*, I told myself.

I started fixing supper, making loud kitchen noises to rouse her. Aunt Mary must still be sleeping. That hog's head I put in the pot this morning did smell good and would taste mighty fine for supper. We hadn't had meat for two days, and I surely was ready for some. I'd cook up some persimmon pudding, too, right now. Aunt Mary might eat some. She'd said the fruit wouldn't pucker up our mouths after we'd had a frost. Even before she got sick, she'd been hungering for that winter treat, and I declare it sounded right tasty. Then too, I'd start some scrapple for tomorrow and mix some dough to set, and then—oh dear. There is so much to do.

I put the persimmons in a pot with a little water. When they were cooked and soft, I'd mash them up for the pudding. I started collecting the ingredients: wheat meal, sugar, eggs if the hens were laying—oh I hoped Uncle Silas would find some in the shed—and milk. It had started to sour, but that was . . .

"Tansy, oh Tansy . . ." I heard Aunt Mary calling from the back room.

"Yes, Ma'am." I pushed open the door. It was pure darkness in there, but I saw glints in Aunt Mary's eyes from the lamp. I fetched it and carried it to her bedside. "Are you well, Aunt Mary?" I peered closely at her.

She struggled to sit up. "Tansy, dear, some water please." Her voice was very weak.

"Yes, ma'am. And some more medicine?"

"Oh Tansy, will I ever feel well, I wonder? Yes, some more laudanum, please. But I dislike it so. It makes me feel sleepy, and then I can't think clearly. How is Letty, my dear baby? And did you have a good walk? Is Mister Cummings in for supper yet? Oh, so much to attend to." She put her feet on the floor, feeling around for her slippers, then held out her pale, trembling hands. "See here, Tansy, I'm not quite so shaky tonight. I think I might go sit in the rocker a bit. Help me, girl."

She was very light, even though she was a tall woman. I helped her into the big room and tucked a quilt about her in the rocker. I spoon-fed her twenty drops of laudanum in a spoonful of whiskey.

"Soon I'll have supper ready, Aunt Mary. Will you eat some tonight?"

"I'll try, dear. I'll try." She grimaced from the taste of the medicine, took a deep breath, and began to rock gently. Just then Letty, across the room in her trundle bed, giggled. "Oh do bring me my baby, Tansy. Come, little child. Your mother wants to hold you." She held her arms out toward the baby.

I brought Letty to Aunt Mary just as she began to cough. This time it went on and on. I stood Letty on the puncheon floor where she held onto her mother's knees and danced up and down, squealing joyfully. Her two new teeth shone from her fetching smile. Aunt Mary's coughing continued until she seemed exhausted. Finally, she leaned over to pick her up, but the effort seemed too great.

"Tansy, please help me. I declare I can't sit up any longer. Oh, dear Lord." She looked heavenward. "Please don't let my child get this sickness."

I helped her into bed and took Letty to change her. What was happening to Aunt Mary? Was she getting well from the ague and now getting consumption? Shouldn't Uncle Silas get the doctor? Would there be no end to this sickness?

I squeezed the seeds out of the persimmons and mashed the pulp. Was I better off here, or should I have slid off the flatboat and drowned, too? That question returned every day to taunt me.

Uncle Silas came in from the shed carrying his hat with three eggs in it. Directly he asked me if I had seen any snakes in town today. I told him no. I wanted to tell him about the strange person I had met, but he went on talking. He said our preacher neighbor down the lane, Elder Jamison, had seen several large, listless snakes. They were coming out of hibernation, way too early. He had seen a deer wandering in town, too. He said it came up close and stood there, unafraid, then bolted across his yard and jumped over his woodpile.

"All kinds of critters been comin' into town—bears, foxes, rabbits—all stayin' together, not afeared of one another, some—their red tongues all hangin' out," Uncle Silas said, talking louder and faster. "I seen 'em too. I even seen two coon chasin' after a deer. Then they stopped right there," he pointed out the door. "And stood still, they did. I was jes' goin for my rifle, when they up and skedaddled, doncha know." He limped to the door of the back room and peered in, then returned to where

I was mixing the fruit pulp with sugar and eggs. I moved away from him. He was too close for my comfort.

"The reverend said there's too much sinnin' goin' on in New Madrid, and God's creation'll feel it first." He paused, staring at me, shook his head and continued. "Then the reverend, he tells me, 'God will punish wickedness,'" said Uncle Silas mockingly. "'All the fightin', mischief, vulgarity, lust, cussin', drinkin', and fornicatin' is goin' to feel God's wrath one day'. Hmmph." Uncle Silas spit into the spittoon, thankfully aiming well this time, hung his coat on a peg, and took off his boots.

"Thunderation!" he continued, "The reverend's lost his head, doncha know. I'm thinkin' he's been whistlin' some. Makes a body hear spirits in the wind, it does."

He poured water into the basin. "What he needs is a nice widder to warm his bed, doncha know. He's got so heavenly minded he ain't no earthly good." He washed his face and hands, slopping water on the floor and leaving the towel grimy. "Where's my girl now? Letty girl? Come see your pa."

Letty crawled across the floor, but stopped midway, holding up her hand, and starting to cry. Her father picked her up and looked at her hand.

"She's got a splinter here, Tansy, off this dad-blamed floor. Git it gone now, quick like." He handed Letty to me. I worked at the splinter and finally managed to lift it out, Letty screaming all the while. She was slobbery with crying, so I fed her some supper, but she whimpered throughout her meal. I dished up some hog meat and broth for me and Uncle Silas. He started eating the minute I put his plate in front of him, paying no further mind to his unhappy child. I peeked in at Aunt Mary, but she was asleep, so I sat down to eat supper, too.

"Whar'd your name, Tansy, come from, girl? Tansy Ragwort's a poison, doncha know. Yessir, it's a poison to cows and horses."

This was the first time Uncle Silas had attempted conversation. I took another taste of broth and put down my spoon. "My mother, Pearl, gave me my name, Uncle Silas. She was named after a flower, Pearly Everlasting, and wanted me to have a flower name too. Most folks we knew in Pennsylvania had sheep, sir, and sheep don't get sick from Tansy Ragwort."

"Pearly Everlasting? She warn't everlasting, now, war she?" He scoffed and wiped his mouth on his sleeve. "Rest her soul. Still and all, it's mighty strange to give a child a poison name, seems like." He picked up his bowl and finished off the broth. He wiped his mouth again and picked up a bone. Great slurps, chomps, and finger-licking soon cleaned it off.

"Best you chew some ginger root, girl, and swaller the juice, doncha know. That'll git yer poison gone. Don't want none of that spillin' onto Letty. Not me and Miz Cummings neither."

Later, when things were tidied up, and Letty was in bed asleep, I sat down in the rocker to sort out my thoughts. Aunt Mary was coughing most harshly and getting worse, I believed. Uncle Silas snored, and I declare, making it hard to think straight.

I hoped Letty wouldn't get sick. She was a healthy, smiling child now. Somehow I wished her a better life than an ailing ma and cantankerous pa. He did love that child, though. Yes he did.

I rocked awhile and hummed a little of *"Barbara Allen."* It made me think about my mama and all the singing times we had. Even after her mind went bad, we still sang, and it was right enjoyable. But Pearly

Everlasting truly hadn't been everlasting, just like Uncle Silas said. I did miss her so, every day.

A cold, vigorous wind had come up suddenly. I could hear it whistling through the walls of this log and clay house. Smoke backed down the brick chimney with each gust, making all of us cough and the room smelly. I added a few logs to the fire and banked it well for the night. Best I went to bed now. I believed it would be icy the next day, and I wondered if the river would freeze.

I took off my apron and slippers and got into my bed. It was so cold tonight, I left my cap on, and my stockings, too. Pulling my long sleeves down over my hands, I curled into a ball, and shivered until warmth crept over me.

As sleepiness followed the warmth, I thought about Solomon. Where was he tonight? Did he have a blanket or a place to sleep? He had no shoes. Although I tried to shake off my thoughts and concerns, they seemed to pile one on another, and I became wakeful. Tomorrow, when I took some pudding to the Southwards, I would take some to Solomon—and a blanket, too, if I could. Maybe Elder Jamison had one I could borrow. I didn't want to ask Uncle Silas.

The wind howled, the fire burned low, the smell of the river invaded the room on waves of cold air. "*Tansy, Tansy Ragwort,*" I murmured. Was I a poison? Good for nothing but harm? What should I do here? These thoughts sent sleep far away, and warm tears spilling from my eyes. I turned toward the wall and cried silently into the night.

* * *

CHAPTER 6

MID-DECEMBER 1811

Aunt Mary was still coughing. None of us slept very well except Letty. Uncle Silas had likely been up and out for a long time. He'd stirred the fire and put some water on to heat. I sliced the scrapple, dipped it in some wheatflour and fried it in hog fat for our breakfast. We were getting low on tea and sugar, so later I'd go down to the dock to see if our supplies had arrived. Of course that meant Uncle Silas would be getting some whiskey. I sorely wished he didn't drink it so often, since that made him more cantankerous than usual.

Letty was wet and her bedding soaked too. I'd need to do a washing today. My poor hands would get so red with painful blisters after scrubbing on that washboard, but wash I must. I hoped there'd be no rain, so things could dry outside.

After eating, I went out to pump more water. It took four bucketfuls before I swung the pot over the fire to heat. I'd need the kettle clear full to wash all the bedding. I added more logs to increase the flames. It was so cold today. A long winter was ahead, I feared.

After attending to Aunt Mary, I fed Letty. Then we bundled up and went outside to say good morning to Mr.

Joe. My foggy breath grew a small cloud when I whistled for him, but he was nowhere to be seen.

Just then Uncle Silas came limping around the side of the house and scowled at me.

"Whistlin' gals and cacklin' hens always comes to some bad ends, doncha know? I'm tellin' you, Poison Girl, you'd best watch your ways." Uncle Silas was wobbling as he walked. I knew his gimpy leg from an arrow wound bothered him, but I guessed he'd been into his whiskey already this morning. He piled a load of wood in his arms and limped inside.

Poison Girl, he'd called me. I wondered, was I really Poison Girl?

Letty squealed, looking up in the persimmon tree.

"No Mr. Joe today, Letty," I told her. I scattered some corn on the frosty ground. Just then a flock of birds I'd never seen before swooped down onto the woodpile and even on us. Letty and I both swished our hands, shooing them away. How strange for birds to land right on our heads.

They ate and ate until a whole flock of those beautiful Carolina Parrots descended, frightening the smaller birds away. Such a large number today! And so close. Strange things were going on around here lately. I sat down on the chopping block with Letty on my lap. What a sight were these small, green birds! Reaching in my pocket I threw out more corn, but they didn't touch it.

We sat watching them peck, peck, peck at various seeds and listening to their chatter. I heard a dog, or maybe a coyote howling in the distance. The howl changed to a low moan. Could that be Elder Jamison's dog? The sound seemed to come from farther away. While I pondered this, a wondrously huge stag bounded in from the forest. He startled me so, I hugged Letty tightly. He halted and seemed to stare at me. I felt no fear, even though he was very large. The howling began again, and the stag disappeared. These peculiar happenings gave me an unsettled feeling.

Oh pshaw! I'd nearly forgotten about Solomon what with washing, cooking, and tending to this family. While Letty was napping, I'd just put some cold johnnycake and the last of the pudding in a basket and start off for the harbor.

"Aunt Mary, do you need anything before I go for supplies?"

"No, Tansy girl." She sounded tired. "You go now, and ask Mr. Cummings if he would take you in the wagon. I do need more of the laudanum, and it should have arrived by now. Didn't we order it last month? There should be coffee, too, and flour and sugar—too much for you to tote home by yourself." Her voice weakened. "But do not tarry long, Dear. I'll try to sleep a bit while you're gone." Aunt Mary coughed long and hard, then sank back onto the pillow. I worried about her anew.

Taking a large basket, I bundled up in an extra shawl, and stepped outside. I felt unsettled about riding with my uncle, but I knew I must obey Aunt Mary. Light snow was falling. Across the lane, I saw Uncle Silas speaking with Elder Jamison. I supposed they talked about the weather and the strange antics of animals lately. The reverend was slim, and taller than my uncle, and leaned over slightly when talking. His large dog, Rufus, sat between them, his tail wagging a fan-shaped path in the dirt, eyes alert watching the forest. His brown and white winter coat stood out stiffly, as if he were nervously awaiting trouble.

I approached and could hear Elder Jamison saying, "The phenomena portend disaster, dear sir, and the population must needs be in attendance at the house of God to hear the Word which is efficacious for instruction, correction, and . . . ."

Uncle Silas interrupted impatiently. "Usin' high falutin' words won't make it happen, Reverend. My missus is doin' poorly, doncha know, and I have a little one too, and now another mouth to feed." He added that last when he noticed me approaching and spat on the ground.

"Brother Cummings," Elder Jamison went on, "do abandon your drinking of spirits and entertain a renewed proclivity regarding Sunday worship. I cannot say your good lady will recover if you continue . . . Oh, good day, Missy." He lifted his hat, bowing slightly to me.

"Good day, Reverend," I said shyly, looking down. I suddenly felt very timid and knew not what to say or do.

"This here's Poison Girl, Reverend," Uncle Silas said. "She's headin' us for trouble, 'deed she is. 'Ceptin' for helpin' out some, she's trouble all right."

"My good man that simply cannot be. Why this innocent child, like the dew on roses, appears to be of sound mind and body." Elder Jamison looked at me and flushed.

"Got quirks about whistlin' and singin' and feedin' our corn to the dad-blamed crows." Turning to me, he said, "So what you standin' here for, Tansy Ragwort? Cat got your tongue?"

"Aunt Mary wants you to take me down to the harbor to collect our supplies, Uncle Silas. She's coughing badly and needs her medicine."

"She says so, does she? Must be gettin' better, that woman. Well, I'll git the wagon and we'll be off before this snow gets to pilin' up." He limped off toward the house, and I was left alone facing Elder Jamison. I felt so, so—I didn't know what—conspicuous, I guess. I tried to escape, but Rufus trotted over to my basket and began sniffing it. I turned around, not wanting him to get at Solomon's food, but he followed me around and around several times.

"No, Rufus, no! Forgive him, dear girl." Elder Jamison grabbed his dog, and they both circled me a few times while I held the basket up high, out of Rufus' reach. In the melee, I knocked Elder Jamison's hat off. Rufus sniffed it several times, clamped it in his teeth, and began chewing. I was sure I saw a look of mischief on his face.

"Fine day, Miss Tansy, wouldn't you agree?" Elder Jamison tried to maintain his dignity while wrenching his hat from the dog's jaws. Finally he succeeded and plunked it back on his head, flattened, and with dirt and dried leaves stuck on with Rufus' slobber. It presented such a humorous scene., I found it hard to speak for the giggles I could barely squelch.

"Yes, indeed, Reverend Jamison," I replied, but I felt all tickly inside and turned and ran toward the wagon Uncle Silas was driving up from the barn. As I climbed in, I laughed out loud—the first time since arriving in Missouri Territory.

Now that Uncle Silas was taking me to the harbor instead of going alone, I fretted about meeting Solomon. I wanted to give him the food I had brought, but Uncle Silas was not kindly disposed toward Negroes, and I was afraid he would give me grief for bringing Solomon food, or even speaking to him. It was a worrisome ride as we bumped along through town. I was mighty relieved, though saddened, that we saw nary a sign of Solomon as we passed through the woods where I had last met him.

As we came up over the rise, the harbor below looked cold and chaotic. Many boats were tied close together, others were anchored offshore. Dogs, horses, chickens, pigs, and boatmen made such a clamor; I could barely take it all in. The smells of pine, whiskey, tobacco, hemp, and manure mingled in the air.

We pulled up next to a flatboat tied by the shore. Maxwell jittered around trying to back away from the water, but Uncle Silas grabbed his bridle and pulled his stubborn mule forward until he stopped beside the loading ramp. He waggled his long ears when Uncle Silas shouted some harsh words at him, but they seemed effectual, all right.

Uncle Silas dealt with the boatmen about the supplies he had ordered. He watched and counted as they were loaded into our wagon. A dozen squabbling, crowing roosters in wooden cages were unloaded, then stacked in with the supplies, adding to the ruckus. Uncle Silas had been waiting for them to replace the ones killed in the last few cockfights.

Our supply of sugar was less than we had ordered, and Uncle Silas complained loudly. I was glad to see a parcel marked, Laudanum Powder—one pound.

"Outright stolen, Mr. Cummings." A crewman said. "Some rapscallion came aboard in the night and stole sugar, 'taters, and even snagged a mug of cold coffee left on the deck. Piles on our agony, sure enough does." The boatman blew his nose. "We seen a lad of color skulking round the docks yest'day. Most likely a runaway."

"No he's not," I said, before I even thought to keep silent. I had told Solomon to ask the boatmen for some food, but I hadn't meant he should steal it! That's what made me speak so suddenly. I was sure Solomon was the "rapscallion."

"What you know about runaways, Missy?" The boatman looked at me with amusement.

"Oh, nothing, Sir. But some people of color are free. That's what I meant." I glanced at Uncle Silas to see if he was listening, but he was tying down the barrels and cages.

The next days fairly raced by with unpacking and storing the supplies, minding Letty, cooking, fetching water, and a hundred other things. Aunt Mary was up and about one or two hours each day and still coughing, but feeling stronger. Letty was standing by herself now before falling on the uneven floor and crying, then laughing while tears ran down her cheeks. Her antics were the cause of some welcome joy in this solemn house. Uncle Silas played pat-a-cake with her in the evenings, and he was, surprisingly, right pleasant at those times.

Cold weather finally came to stay in New Madrid. Most days were clear and frosty, but snow or icy drizzle appeared often enough. Those sunless days cast a gloom in this house that dulled my sensibilities. When the sun did come out, it was fiery red lately, and no one knew why. The comet still gave its dim glow, but we all grew used to it after a while and paid it little heed. Since nothing happened in the way of disaster, Uncle Silas didn't talk much about it being a bad omen anymore.

I picked up some more wild persimmons after a hard freeze, and now that we had sugar, the puddings were sweet and tasty. Letty fussed for more when her portion was gone, but I didn't want her to get sickly from too much fruit, so I wouldn't give in to her complaint. I usually sang to her about swinging in the apple tree but I sang persimmon tree and rocked her some, and she usually stopped crying.

Aunt Mary and I commenced talking together when my chores were done, and she was sitting up in the rocking chair. She remarked about this "year of extraordinaries" as she called it. We counted up all the strange happenings that had been going on for some time now: the comet, the squirrels all drowning themselves in the Ohio River, and the eclipse of the sun.

Aunt Mary told me about last year—the "year of many waters" the Indians had called it, when spring floods on the rivers were worse than anyone could remember. Uncle Silas had to replant the corn after the first planting was washed away.

"And I can't forget losing my father last winter in Pennsylvania, and my mother and brothers this past summer," I said. "Mostly that's what makes this year so hard to bear. I do hope that's the end of extraordinaries, Aunt Mary. I'm glad you're getting well and that this year is finally coming to an end."

* * *

CHAPTER 7

DECEMBER 16, 1811

Just before I fell asleep, my thoughts wandered back through the day. I thought about my talk with Aunt Mary. Somehow I felt closer to her than ever. There seemed to be a welcome tranquility in the house tonight. Maybe I'd get peaceable living here after all. The fire crackled, sending dancing lights across the room. An owl hooted outside, the faint murmur of the river was soothing, and I was soon asleep.

Sometime later, in the middle of the night, a tremendous noise wakened me, like the loudest thunder I'd ever heard. Startled, I sat up in my bed, pulling a blanket around my shoulders. Just then the floor rose up right before me and tilted sideways, and the whole room shuddered. Fear gripped me fiercely, and my breathing nearly stopped. Bricks from the fireplace tumbled down. A burning log rolled out onto the puncheon floor.

"Oh! Help!" I shouted. I dashed across the room but with great difficulty, for the floor was rocking. Grabbing the poker, I struggled to push the log back into the fireplace. The kettle had fallen down, too, and bricks were clunking into it. Suddenly the whole chimney collapsed, and I was left looking through dust and smoke to the outside. Trees were waving and snapping, and lights were flashing. And the noise! Like hoarse roaring! A shrill whistle pierced the night.

"Aunt Mary," I screamed. "What is happening?" I must get to Letty! Or should I see about Aunt Mary? The house gave another lurch. I fell against the wall and pain pierced my shoulder. Fear welled up in my throat and choked me, and cold perspiration broke out over my whole body. Aunt Mary was moaning. Was she hurt?

"Oh, Aunt Mary! Letty! Are you safe?" I yelled into the darkness.

"Earthquake!" shouted Uncle Silas. He staggered from the back room in his night shirt and cap, and fell to his knees. He got up, but was thrown back down as the floor heaved and the walls shook. Up again, he struggled past me, climbing over upturned furniture. The door swung open by itself, and he stumbled outside. He fell again, got up on his knees, raised his arms in the air and shouted, "He done it! God done it to us. The reverend was right. We're being punished for our sins!" He fell on his face sobbing as the ground pitched him up and down.

A terrible odor filled the room. I had to force breaths into my lungs, for they wouldn't take in enough air, whether from the acrid smell or my own fear, I couldn't tell. The sound of cracking trees, the horrid vapor, the pitch darkness between flashes of lightning, the icy air coming in the open door and where the fireplace had been . . . .

I finally reached Letty who was, strangely, still asleep. Just then the house lifted slightly, and I fell over the rocking chair onto a broken lamp. Glass cut my hand, and warm blood soaked into my sleeve. Oh what should I do? I couldn't see! My head pounded—I must have bumped it hard. My breath came in shallow gulps.

"Aunt Mary?" I called, crawling on my hands and knees toward the back room. "Are you hurt, Aunt Mary?" I heard only a weak groan.

"I'm coming, Aunt Mary! I'm coming!"

I made my way into the back room just as another tremor began. Thankfully, she was not hurt, just badly frightened. I struggled back to the door to see about Uncle Silas. Dim shapes raced past the house! Voices called out! Animals howled! When lightning flashed, I saw a bear lumber out of the woods adding to my fear. I saw our mule and pigs dash away in different directions. The chickens flapped and squawked and flew up and around and into each other.

The rest of the night I crawled about checking on the devastation. Uncle Silas did not return, and I lost track of time, but eventually slept some and finally awoke enough to welcome some daylight. Letty was awake too. I could hear her tossing in her bed. My shift was stuck to my arm with dried blood! What happened? Oh yes, I remember. I had cut myself . . . yes, yes, there was an earthquake. The lamp had fallen, and I had fallen on the broken glass. My fingers probed above my left eye and discovered a huge lump, and it hurt when I touched it. And oh! Aunt Mary! I must go and see to her. But then the floor rolled again! Had it done this all night?

"Letty, you wait for Cousin Tansy," I called to the baby. "I'll get you presently!" I got up, feeling somewhat dizzy, but made my way around the broken glass, setting the dented lamp up on the flour bin. Everything was upside down and scattered. Oh! Oh! Oh! I recalled Uncle Silas groping across the room. I had to see to him too. He had gone out the door, and it was hanging by one hinge.

Again the house danced to and fro. The foul smell returned, making it hard to breathe. Out the window, which was cracked, some sort of dark liquid was spurting into the air. And where did that round hole come from? It was never there before. The earth must be sinking!

"Help!" I cried. Oh, I was so frightened! I grasped the shaking wall to steady myself. Just then the room became dark! "Aunt Mary! Where are you? Do speak to me!"

The hazy, morning light returned as quickly as it had disappeared, and the rocking of the house ceased, but not before I saw Aunt Mary being bounced about in her bed. I rushed to her side and placed my hands on each side of her face. "Speak to me, Aunt Mary. Please!"

She opened her eyes. They had a look of desperation; her mouth formed words with no sound. I rolled her head back and forth. "Do speak to me! Please do," I implored. She continued to mouth words, but only anguished cries came forth. Her arms reached out as her horrified gaze fixed on my bruised forehead.

"This is nothing," I told her, brushing hair away from the bump. "I will bring Letty to you, so you can nurse her," I said hopefully. "She will bring words from you." I retraced my path and picked up Letty, who smiled sleepily at me as I carried her to the back room.

"Ooh," she said solemnly, touching my lumpy bruise with a pudgy finger.

"Don't worry, Letty girl. Here's your mama. Can you give her some love?" I put Letty down on Aunt Mary's bed. She hugged her mother, whose anxious face softened at the sight of her daughter.

"I'll go see about Uncle Silas," I told her.

I threaded my way across both rooms, avoiding the broken glass, righting chairs and the table. I struggled through the dangling door, and looked up and down the lane. Uncle Silas was nowhere to be seen. But I saw many houses in woeful condition. The Adler's brick house was flattened; the next one had two walls missing. Many homes were tilted to one side. Piles of bricks smoldered where once fires had warmed sleeping families, their chimneys now destroyed.

Stepping into the lane, I saw the crumpled church steeple astride some rubble where the church had been, its cross still upright. In places the land had sunk; some holes were filled with water or with sand. And there! There were mounds where none had been before, and oh, trees were down everywhere, just everywhere!

Neighbors were milling about or running toward the edge of town; some in clusters, some alone. Fearful voices were shouting, children were crying. I still did not see Uncle Silas.

Rufus came dashing from Elder Jamison's lop-sided house, whining, his tongue hanging out. He jittered around me, stepping on my bare feet. I didn't know why. I certainly couldn't help him. He started back toward his house, then sat down and howled. He wanted something, but I needed to find Uncle Silas; and I needed to go back to my own house. My feet were numbing with the cold.

As I started away, Rufus howled and barked again. Maybe he was telling me something. I turned back and followed him to the reverend's house.

Through a cracked window, I saw Elder Jamison's head sticking out from under a heap of broken furniture wedged under the leaning wall. Books were scattered everywhere. Was he dead? I tapped on the window. He looked up and began speaking in dignified phrases, as if he were not hurt, just out of breath.

"Please be so kind—dear lady—to hasten inside—and render me some assistance."

Rufus, half inside the open door, was panting. I saw immediately what must be done. I began removing furniture until the reverend was able to sit up, take a deep breath, and say, "Most gracious salutations, Miss Tansy, is it?"

I nodded, yes.

He stood awkwardly and continued, "See what God hath wrought, my lady? Two violent earthquakes, and I've counted eighteen smaller ones since the first trembler brought the wall down upon me. Oh, what is man, that God is mindful of him? Just observe . . ." He spread his hands out to indicate the fallen chimney, the broken furniture, a missing wall, its stone remains scattered out over the woodpile.

Rufus emitted a low growl, his lips curling back over his teeth. He looked quite fearsome. The dog frightened me, and I wanted nothing more than to be away from him, from the earthquake, from this terrifying time. I hastened outside. Animals from the woods were wandering through town. A wolf was sitting on his haunches staring into a pool of putrid water. A bear lumbered past again, giving me the shivers. Several deer dashed here and there, and turkeys, gobbling nervously, ran after the deer, then after the bear. Rufus continued growling, staying behind me; his eyes following each animal's antics.

I stepped back in the house. "I nearly forgot, Elder Jamison," I said. "Have you seen Mr. Cummings? He ran out of the house last night and hasn't come back."

"Nay, dear lady. I have neither seen nor heard from the kind gentleman. Your uncle, I believe?"

"Yes, Sir, he is my Uncle Silas. Aunt Mary is feeling so poorly, and the baby is . . . . Oh I must go now."

I started toward home, stepping carefully around the clutter in the lane. I saw Miss Wilson, the school marm, climbing over a fallen tree. She was tugging angrily at her skirt that was caught on a branch, the soft gray homespun shredding as she pulled. All the while she vainly tried to maintain her modesty, seemingly more distressed over her ankle being visible, than over the earthquake's chaos or a torn dress.

"Miss Squires!" she snapped. "Kindly help me, won't you?" I heard my surname so infrequently, I looked around to see whom she was addressing. Seeing her predicament, I ran quickly to loosen her skirt from the branch, and she scooted to the ground.

"Isn't this most dreadful, Miss Squires? Are you and your family surviving this disaster, my dear?" As her anger faded, she looked genuinely concerned when I told her of Aunt Mary's condition and about the house.

"And Uncle Silas is nowhere to be seen, Mistress Wilson. Have you yourself seen him?"

"I declare, no. I've been quite busy gathering news from others of the immense damage inflicted upon this town, God save us. Oh, such calamities! Oh, oh, oh!" Miss Wilson fell into step beside me and continued. "Did you hear about the ground opening up, and a stranger falling into it before it closed over his head? Or did you know, my dear, that the banks of the graveyard—oh it's too awful to speak about—but they have fallen into the river, and coffins too! Oh, yes." She leaned toward me, so close I felt her breath on my face. "Bodies emerged when the coffins fell into the water and floated away down the river!" She took a deep breath. "And the Indian villages along the river . . . , oh it's too dreadful. Not a soul left in them. All those little savages . . . ." She seemed to need to talk, for she went on and on, faster and faster.

Clouds gathered as we walked; the air was chill. My bare feet were stiff and numb with cold. Again the ground rolled beneath us, trees swayed, branches fell. I bumped into Miss Wilson and fell into the path. Before I could get up, this proper lady hastily covered my feet with my skirt, for just then, we saw Solomon coming from the direction of the river, his turban askew, breeches and shirt stained and torn. A wooden shingle was sticking out of his shirt. He smiled vacantly when he saw me. "Solomon hungry. Want food," he said. Had it been several days since our first meeting? This sounded like a continuation of our last conversation. While he was speaking thus, he dropped the shingle to the ground, and stepped on it with his bare feet.

"Whatever are you doing, young man?" Miss Wilson demanded.

"Warm feet," Solomon said. "Make warm feet." He smiled again, stood still a few more seconds, then reached down, picked up the shingle and put it back inside his shirt. My own feet were so cold, I wondered if his feet really warmed on that piece of wood.

"Come, Solomon. I will give you some food." I pointed toward our house and started in that direction, and he followed. Miss Wilson turned and bid us good health, still talking. I heard the words "chimneys," "sand boils," "folks and animals running in and out of the woods." Her words grew fainter, until she climbed over another downed tree and was out of earshot.

Another strong jolt announced itself with a loud "crack," throwing me down on the ground again. Solomon fell too, quickly pulling out his shingle and sliding it under his knees. Loud cries from all around accompanied the shaking earth. I scrambled down the cluttered lane, over the doorsill and into the house, calling for Letty and Aunt Mary. The house rocked back and forth, then stopped quite suddenly.

"Oh these horrid quakes!" Aunt Mary shouted from the back room. She was standing up, holding Letty, and came stumbling into the front room. When she saw all the damage, and the absence of the chimney, she cried loudly, "What shall we do? What ever shall we do, Tansy? And where is Mr. Cummings?" She looked at Solomon, who had followed me inside. "And who is this?"

"This is Solomon, Aunt Mary," I said.

"This is Solomon," repeated Solomon, smiling, and holding out the shingle to Letty.

At that moment, Elder Jamison burst into the room, Rufus following on his heels. "Snake!" he called hoarsely. "There's a copperhead in my house!" He stopped short, seeing Aunt Mary. "Good day, Mrs. Cummings. Do forgive my excitable state." He removed his hat and stood rigid, although his hands, rotating his hat round and round, trembled slightly.

As I took in all these happenings, one on top of another, Solomon suddenly grabbed the ham still hanging from the ceiling timber, and dashed out the door. Before we could speak, Rufus barked long and loud at the retreating thief, then sidled up to his master and sat down as if waiting for a reward. No one spoke. I certainly could not think what to say or do. I just looked from one to the other. Aunt Mary sat down in the rocker and stared straight ahead. Elder Jamison rotated his hat. Letty giggled and clapped her hands, as if all this chaos was merriment just for her.

* * *

CHAPTER 8

LATE DECEMBER 1811

December had finally settled itself into a nearly constant, cold drizzle. Nights were frosty, and snow flurries came and went. Some days warmed up a bit, but most were miserably cold. The animals' water troughs were often ice-covered. I dealt with the situation the best I could. A fire in the chimney rubble gave a bit of warmth in the house and allowed me to melt ice so the animals could have water. I was kept busy washing clothes for Letty—how dirty that baby could get! Hot water and then scrubbing hard on the washboard made my hands raw and red. If I rubbed a little pork fat on my hands they softened some, but then oh how they smelled!

Uncle Silas had not been seen since that dreadful night of the first earthquake. Although Aunt Mary was despondent, she had improved somewhat. She was able to care for Letty most days while I cleaned, cooked, and cared for the animals.

It was tiring work. With the fallen bricks I built up a wall of sorts to keep the fire contained and Letty away from it. Her antics kept Aunt Mary and me from crying all the time, although we did spend some tearful times in that state. Everything seemed so terrible. Where would this all end?

We felt rumblings almost every day. So many folks had left town. It seemed like a stream of carts, dogs, horses, mules and families passed our house each day. Maybe we should have gone too, but where? And with Aunt Mary so weak, and the baby to carry and all . . . . Anyway, Aunt Mary said to stay here, for she was sure Uncle Silas would return. Although life was hard without him, and I didn't know how to care for the animals so well, yet I sometimes hoped he wouldn't come back.

Elder Jamison stayed in a protected corner of his house down the lane, and Rufus guarded him against wild animals and snakes. He was very helpful to us. The reverend fixed our brick chimney today so less cold air and rain came in. He had been taking some meals with us, bringing in extras like onions and potatoes. They were gratefully received, for our potatoes had all rotted this winter. He even brought rice and sassafras one day, and with our hog meat and hominy, he showed me how to make a stew he called gumbo. He had traveled to New Orleans some time back and learned to eat it there. It tasted mighty queer, I decided. But Aunt Mary and I found it tolerable, however, Letty would have none of it.

I kept wondering what each day would bring. Is this what my life would be from now on? Long, dark days all the same?

One day, before fixing supper, I sat in the rocker and picked up my sampler to work on. The numbers were nearly finished, and soon I could start embroidering the Bible verse. I still couldn't remember the word that was so faint and hard to read. I would ask Elder Jamison next time I saw him. I began to sing an old song:

> *I'm just a poor wayfarin' stranger*
> *a travelin' through this world of woe . . .*

Before I finished the song, I was nodding off. I awakened smiling. I'd been dreaming about springtime with blooming redbud and dogwood trees brightening up the forest. I crept into my bed, hoping I could refresh the dream while I slept. I closed my eyes and ordered the picture of springtime back into my senses. I breathed deeply to capture the season. Soon sleep crept upon me, and this quiet pleasure sent me into a dreamland again with no cold room, sickness, deserters, wild animals, quaking earth, or destroyed houses.

Morning came and with it hard, cold reality. This was still winter in Missouri, not the place of my dreams. Oh, how I would miss springtime in Pennsylvania. I hoped a Missouri spring would be as nice when the weather warmed up from this dismal gray cold. Maybe Mr. Joe would come back when the fruit trees blossomed and the fragrance would blow in on rustling leaves.

"*Rouse yourself, Tansy,*" I said, turning over. I had fallen back asleep in morning's broad daylight, and with chores awaiting me, too. "*It's time to get up, Lazybones.*"

I stretched and yawned, but was startled into complete wakefulness—by what? Another earthquake? No. I heard voices! And footsteps! I jumped up, grabbed my shawl, and peeked out the door. On the gravel path, an Indian, dressed in buckskin with a rough wool blanket about his shoulders, was walking toward our house. Mistress Wilson was hurrying to keep up with him. She was talking fast, though he seemed to pay little attention. Dangling by their feet, their heads and wattles dragging on the ground, were two very dead turkeys. At the sight, my breath caught in my throat.

"Mistress Wilson," I called. "Do you need help?" I sounded more courageous than I felt, for I wondered if this Indian was dangerous.

She glanced my way. "Good day, Miss Squires. Nay, I need no help from you. I am asking this savage if I may purchase one of his birds here." She reached for one of the turkeys, but the Indian continued his long strides, keeping them out of her reach. I walked toward the two visitors cautiously.

I had heard the boatmen down at the harbor speak to Indians who wanted to trade with them for tobacco or liquor. I cleared my throat and spoke bravely.

"Peace, Brother. Will you sell turkey to woman?" I nodded at Mistress Wilson.

"I bring you turkeys." He indicated my house. "Solomon say good white woman here." He pushed past Mistress Wilson roughly, and dropped the two fowl in my arms. I staggered backwards, grasping my shawl and the two turkeys and nearly losing my balance. I was so astonished my mind spun with a thousand thoughts, but no words. Whatever did this mean? Solomon, who stole our ham, sent this Indian to give me turkeys? And Mistress Wilson standing here ready to plank down some cash, jabbering some nonsense about this savage and why she should have a turkey. But I was attentive to the man before me.

"Who are you, Brother?" I asked. "Why do you bring me turkeys? Where is Solomon?" I shivered as the wind blew my skirts around me. A light snow had begun to fall, coating us all with lacy flakes.

"Shawnee man, Running Wolf. Me hunt food. Find Solomon. He say take wild turkey to white woman in wood house by persimmon tree."

I did not understand this native before me very well, but I said, "I will take the food. Thank you. Please tell your people Tansy Squires is friend to Running Wolf."

"Running Wolf lose many people. Great Water take village. Many brothers die. Long Knives not die. Great Spirit good to Long Knives. Now Running Wolf find new village and family here? Sister of Tecumseh live here with husband, Francois Maisonville. Do you know?"

"I know Monsieur Maisonville. His house is beyond Mistress Wilson's, along the bayou where . . ." I tried to finish, but Mistress Wilson interrupted.

"It's beyond the schoolhouse by the millrace. Such a civilized lady is Madame Maisonville. And such nice children too. They always do their lessons and say please and thankee." Mistress Wilson talked on and on.

My teeth were chattering, for my shawl was very thin, and even though I wished to stay and hear more, I bid good day. Running Wolf followed me, making me somewhat nervous. I dashed inside the house to get warm and closed the door.

Later, as I was standing close to the fireplace and rubbing my cold hands, Mistress Wilson knocked on the door, calling out as she stepped inside. "Would you care to give me one of those turkeys, Miss Squires? 'Twould be so neighborly of you."

I told her no, but invited her to join us for Christmas Eve when we should roast and serve turkey. She eagerly agreed, then plunged into another subject.

"Did you hear the steamboat going past on the river today, my dear? Oh, it was so loud! It clattered and smoked. It fairly swept down the river. Just this morning, it was. Just imagine, a boat operated by steam!"

"No, Ma'am, I did not hear it. What is a steamboat?" I wondered if she ever stopped talking.

"Why, my dear, they say it's a boat with a contraption full of fire that makes steam, which turns a huge paddle. Why, I could see it from my house. It went so fast. Yes, it was faster than the river was flowing! Oh, what will they invent next?" She halted briefly to catch her breath, then began again with renewed vigor.

"When I went to the harbor yesterday, I heard the boatmen say that the steamboat would arrive right here in New Madrid today, so I was watching for it, yes I was." She shook her head sadly and took a breath. "But it did not stop here."

Brightening again, she went on. "Oh, it was huge, and clackety-clack it came, and there was a woman on it! Just imagine! And she had a baby and a dog and a cabin, and even plants in the windows." Her voice became louder and shriller. "And she waved! And I hear tell that boat can go upstream too! Just imagine, Miss Squires. A boat that can travel upstream, that you need not row! Why, all those flatboats and keelboats will soon be out of date, I declare." At this, she took another breath and stopped speaking. For a moment, anyway.

Letty crawled into the room and, seeing Mistress Wilson, stopped and stared, her blue eyes taking in the stranger with infant curiosity.

"Why I declare, just look at that baby. My, how she has grown!"

"Will you drink a cup of tea, Mistress Wilson?" Aunt Mary had come from the back room and greeted the guest with the invitation.

Looking a bit annoyed at being interrupted, until she saw who was talking, Mistress Wilson replied, "I will indeed, Mistress Cummings. How kind of you to ask." She looked for a place to sit, eyed the rocker, and plunked herself down.

I brewed and served a pot of tea, using Aunt Mary's English china cups. Mistress Wilson noted a chipped edge and lamented the broken teacups in her own house. I wrapped Letty in a blanket, and putting on another shawl, took her outside to let the two ladies talk. Perhaps it was one lady talk and one lady listen, I thought, pulling the door closed behind me.

As the cold air hit her face, Letty squealed and grabbed me around the neck. I pointed to the bare tree.

"Look up yonder, Letty." There sat Mr. Joe. After all these days, he was back again! We welcomed him, and I tossed him some corn from my pocket. He flitted down to peck at it, tipping his head sideways and keeping watch on us with one black eye as he pecked at the grain.

Aunt Mary, though up and around, often sighed long and loud, shivering in her shift, shawl, and cap. And I, I felt lightened spirits only when Letty was playing with her cup or rag doll or some chicken feathers I brought in from the shed. But most times I fretted about keeping us all warm and fed, things I never concerned myself about back in Pennsylvania. Food supplies were running short now, and I knew not where more would come from.

Aunt Mary and I wondered where Uncle Silas was. Even with him gone, his influence remained. I still felt his disapproval, his criticism; his superstitions still stabbed me when I whistled or took Letty outside or saw my reflection in the window. Sometimes I thought Aunt Mary didn't miss him at all. I didn't, but then I felt guilty, for he was sorely needed. Other menfolk had also disappeared from New Madrid since the earthquakes, and many families were in worse predicaments than we were.

After Letty was in bed, Aunt Mary and I sometimes talked about her past. She had been to school in France as a young girl and learned to read and to play the clavichord. She told me again about a fancy dress-up ball where she met Thomas Jefferson, "back in the old days. They were so fine—the parties, the shopping, the food—Ah Paree!" she said with a faraway look and faint smile. She stopped rocking and sat up straight. "But I didn't dance with him," she said. Did I perceive a touch of regret in her voice?

She went on, "About that time, my father thought this young country would be a good place to raise your mother, Tansy, so we came to America. She was only ten, but already looking forward to being out and about like I was. Also, I heard Papa tell our mother he wanted me to marry an American. He thought the French suitors were too interested in parties and fine clothes. 'Mary should marry a hard worker,' he said." And so I did. But he was a Frenchman after all!" Aunt Mary chuckled at the remembrance.

She told me how she lost Uncle Pierre in the war. Then she had been all alone and not able to keep the farm going in Pennsylvania. Uncle Silas was a worker on her farm, and when he decided to come to New Madrid with the group of people who were going to settle the town for Spain, he told her to come too, for he needed a wife. She needed a new life, so she married him and came with him.

"Did you love him, Aunt Mary?" I asked. "Mama thought so, but did you?" Aunt Mary pursed her lips and was silent. I wished I hadn't asked her such a question.

* * *

CHAPTER 9

DECEMBER 24, 1811 INTO JANUARY 1812

Christmas Eve dinner was cooking; extra candles had been lit; and that night we tried to remember some of the joys of the season. It seemed unlikely, for holiday pleasures were far in the past for me; perhaps they would never come again. But by late afternoon, when the sky was nearly dark, I couldn't help feeling a bit festive. I had made an apple cake and sweetened it with molasses that Elder Jamison had brought us. He was coming for supper, and Mistress Wilson was already here to celebrate the Lord's birth.

A murmur of voices outside halted our preparations. It was too early for the reverend to be arriving. I went to the door and looked outside. A rabble of folks, maybe twenty or thirty, were staggering down the lane crying, and calling out for help. Whatever was this disturbance? I wrapped my shawl about my shoulders and went outside.

Elder Jamison and other townsfolk were trying to hear from several of the ragged, soaking wet, wild-eyed people all talking at once!

"We have walked twenty-six miles from Little Prairie!" someone shouted to anyone who would listen.

"Our town is no more!" another said. "Earthquakes have swallowed it up!"

From all around voices were wailing, murmuring, and calling out for food or shelter or help of any kind. Some ran one way or another; others dragged their feet, carrying whimpering babies or soaking wet parcels. Freezing rain pelted the crowd. Sopping wind swished against me, and I cowered back into the dry house.

"Just listen, Mistress Wilson," I said. "These people are in dire trouble." Again, voices rose above the tumult.

"We need dry clothes!"

"We have waded through swamps and fallen into sink holes!"

"We have tripped over downed trees!"

"Our children are tired and wet!"

"Our old folks can barely walk!"

"The ground opened! It swallowed a black man!"

"We need help!"

The crowd of desperate Little Prairie refugees eventually thinned out, some finding shelter with relatives, some with friends, some with strangers. I asked Aunt Mary if three little children, who seemed to be alone, might sleep before the fireplace in our house, and she was agreeable. We had hardly blankets enough for ourselves, but with Uncle Silas gone, we had an extra. Then too, we had a wolf skin and a bearskin, so the children would be warm enough, crowding together. Poor little ragamuffins. They were so cold and wet, and hungry. I gave them biscuits and coffee, and they dropped off to sleep before I could set the table with three more plates.

The turkeys roasting over the fire were nearly ready, and the aroma filled the room with mouth-watering promise. I gave the spit another crank, and juice fell sputtering into the flames. The squash pie was already on the table.

This was a strange Christmas Eve, not like any I had experienced before. However, I was beginning to feel some pleasure today. Maybe it was just because of the holiday.

Elder Jamison arrived just as supper was ready. He had tucked a sprig of dried oak leaves into the brim of his hat, making him look rather silly, I decided, yet in keeping with the day.

"Greetings and salutations to you, Miss Squires, Mrs. Cummings, Mistress Wilson." He bowed formally to each of us, then straightened up in surprise, seeing the sleeping children on the floor. I explained about our guests. He removed his hat and stamped the snow off his boots, being careful not to splatter the visitors.

"I do declare," he said, "the magnificence of odors emanating from your domicile might bring the entire town and all its pitiful refugees to the door this night." I thought I saw a slight smile from this sedate gentleman, a first time I was able to recall such a wonder.

We sat down around the table. Aunt Mary was holding Letty, who was banging her spoon on her cup. Elder Jamison eyed the table with its bounty, bowed his head, and began to pray in a voice like thunder.

"Almighty and ever-living God, we give thee humble thanks for these thy bountiful gifts set before us. Thou hast graciously provided for our sustenance, and we, though woefully unworthy, gratefully acknowledge thy provision, particularly the squash pie, the mashed turnips, and not forgetting the masterpieces of epicurean delight, the roast turkeys, and at the conclusion of the meal..."

I was astonished at his memory! I opened my eyes, for I thought his prayer was finished, given its length and power and saw that he was looking at the fare on the table.

"And apple cake," he added, closing his eyes and continuing.

"We do most humbly beseech thee on this auspicious occasion, yea, even the anniversary of the birth of thine only son, the Prince of Peace, to bring peace to these thy people in this house, and to all in these wilderness parts, which have undergone continuous evidence of thy wrath. Forgive us our shortcomings for thy dear son's sake. A..."

He paused, and I opened my eyes again ready to pass the food. His eyes were still closed.

"And Father, bless these pitiful little children who have found refuge in this house, innocent victims of the tumult about us. Amen." He promptly began carving the turkey.

Just as we were filling our plates, the door opened and Solomon burst in with Rufus right behind him. He was tattered and dirty and stood still, blinking in the lamplight.

"Christmas," he said with a grin. "Joyful."

"Solomon!" I said. I was glad to see him. "Come and eat—we have turkey. Oh, yes! You knew—you sent them here with Running Wolf. We do thank you."

He sat on the one available chair and reached for the bird, grasping one of its legs. He dragged it across the table, and the leg broke off in his hand, while the rest of the bird slid onto his lap, then onto the floor.

Rufus was at it in a minute, chomping huge bites of the golden-crisp, savory breast. In the ruckus, the three children awakened. Hearing the snarling dog, two of the three began to cry. The third crawled over to the turkey, lifted off a loose piece of meat, and stuffed it into her mouth. Rufus growled and barked at her. Letty began to cry. Elder Jamison grabbed Rufus' collar with one hand and the turkey with the other, upsetting his chair and falling over backwards.

I was stunned and speechless! I looked from one to another, knowing I should do something about Letty, or the turkey, or the three children. But my eyes rested on Solomon, a turkey leg in his mouth, its grease shining on cheeks and chin. His countenance said he was heedless of all but the pleasure of his palate.

I couldn't help myself. I began to laugh. Uncontrollable giggles erupted from deep within me, though I tried hard to quench them. Aunt Mary chuckled, as did the reverend. Mistress Wilson put the turkey back on the table, telling it to stay put for several good reasons that went on and on.

Solomon looked up at me and smiled. "Christmas," he said. "Joyful."

* * *

CHAPTER 10

LATE JANUARY 1812

January came roaring down the Mississippi with blasts of cold air that kept us miserable and busy feeding the hungry fire. While splitting firewood or tending Letty and the three children, it was hard to keep my fingers and toes warm. Occasionally the earth rumbled again, and the walls of the house creaked and moaned, but they stayed up! I was glad this wasn't a brick house. Most of those in the village had collapsed.

We had fewer tremors lately, but every time the floor rolled, Aunt Mary exclaimed, "Glory be!" We all stopped then, frozen in place, wondering if the damage would be worse than the time before. We were hoping these extraordinary events would end soon, and that this new year would be better than the last. If we could just hold out through winter . . . Uncle Silas had cut and stacked plenty of wood, but the pile was dwindling fast—and then what?

Letty had taken a few steps by herself, though she would not be a year old until next month, but the logs of the puncheon floor, being so uneven and all, tripped her sometimes. Then she would fall, and oh, such screams would rock the house—like another earthquake—almost!

And such bruises she had all over her legs, poor little girl.

Aunt Mary said Letty was too young to start being contrary like a two-year-old, but once, when she was taking some steps, the floor began to roll. Well, that was when Letty said her second word: "NO!" she told the floor as she fell. Her first word, "Dada," must mean her papa, Uncle Silas, for she did miss him, I believed. Each time the door opened, she looked expectantly toward it, saying, "Da da da."

Today was January 22 and tomorrow would be my birthday. I'd be fifteen years old. Sometimes I felt like fifty years old, and I must have looked it, too. Lately I'd had an urge to see myself in a mirror. I knew I shouldn't peek into Aunt Mary's trunk where she kept one, but today the desire came so strongly upon me, I succumbed to the temptation. I was also filled with curiosity about that blue velvet redingote. I sometimes daydreamed about how Aunt Mary might have looked in it, all dressed up at a dance, where Mr. Thomas Jefferson was in attendance. Had she shaken hands with him, I wondered? She didn't dance with him, I knew.

Since she felt well enough to feed the chickens and stock this morning and was out in the shed, I hurried into the back room and opened the trunk. Right on top, beside a fan and two books—one was a Bible—lay that beautiful cloak. I touched it over and over, brushing its softness against my cheek. I wondered just how it would look on me with my plain brown hair and hazel eyes. I held it under my chin and picked up the mirror. I hadn't seen my whole face since coming to Missouri. What a surprise! My eyes and hair and heavy eyebrows were just the same, but my forehead and chin were dotted with red bumps! I didn't like their look at all and stuck out my tongue at them. Peering closer, I searched for the freckles I'd always had across my nose, but nary a one did I see today. They must have traded with the red bumps, I guessed.

Oh! Pshaw! Aunt Mary was coming! I closed the trunk quickly and hurried out to the front room.

"Look here, Tansy," she said, a blast of cold air swooshing into the room with her. "Some of the chickens have returned to us and sent you a gift." Aunt Mary held out two eggs. "See that you make a special cake, Dear. For your birthday."

They were warm in my hands. Just the idea of fresh eggs, birthday cake, and spring not far off—well maybe, just maybe, life in Missouri wouldn't be so bad after all.

I awakened the next day with a smile. I had been dreaming about springtime again, and going fishing down at the harbor with Solomon. In my dream he had caught a catfish that meowed as he pulled it in. How silly, I thought, smiling even more.

Suddenly, just as I sat up, the floor rose in front of me. Oh no! Not again! The walls rattled, the door banged opened. I jumped out of bed and rushed to Letty while the house rolled this way and that. Then it sank on one side. Bricks tumbled out of the fireplace again, and walls shook. I ran outside with Letty in my arms. People were crowding into the lanes, shouting in terror. This time the quake seemed as hard as the big one back in December. Trees swayed and cracked; one split right before my eyes. I saw it fall across Elder Jamison's house. Dear me, I hoped he wasn't hurt. A crater opened in the lane directly in front of me, and black, smelly liquid spurted into the air as high as the persimmon tree; then the black stuff showered down all around. The early morning light suddenly darkened; the sky filled with dust and sand and something like charcoal. The noise! Oh, the noise—a roaring and whistling! It went on for two or three minutes it seemed. How fearsome this all was!

Finally it stopped. But trees still tangled and toppled. *This is terrible! We must leave here*, I repeated over and over in my head! I wished I were still in Pennsylvania! I wanted my mother! And my father and brothers!

"I hate Missouri!" I screamed. I stumbled back inside, tears of fear and anger nearly blinding me.

I heard Aunt Mary in the back room crying out, "Glory be! Oh glory glory be!"

"Aunt Mary, we must get away from here. This is no place to stay. Hurry! Let us be gone. Quickly!"

Mistress Wilson came dashing around a crater shouting to everyone. "Get you all out of town! We are not safe anymore! Now! Take only what you can carry. Go to higher ground at Tywappity Hill!"

Panicky townsfolk hurried past our house. I stared after them, trancelike. Men guided donkey or horse carts and wagons around crevices, trees, and spouting water. Most carts were loaded with children, bundles, hams, feed sacks, and small animals, all heading away from town. Screams pierced the air, mingling with a strange, snake-like hissing. A putrid smell, like rotting vegetables or damp smoldering logs, surrounded us in a foul warm mist. Cracks in the ground, suddenly-appearing pools, or toppling trees vied for my attention making me dizzy trying to sort out which would be the least dangerous route for us to take.

Mistress Wilson ran into our house, shouting, "Come, Mrs. Cummings. There are tents and shelters up on Tywappity Hill. You must leave now. More earthquakes are coming, and it will be safe up there." She flew out as rapidly as she had flown in. Far ahead of her, Elder Jamison and the Southward boys were frantically salvaging a cart that was losing its load of supplies. Their mule had stumbled into a crater, and rising water was already up to its belly.

We were dizzy with fear, and leaving home was the only thing impressed upon us at this moment. I scurried the three children into their boots; I draped the animal skins over them, and shooed them out the door.

"Follow the people going that way." I pointed up the lane. Aunt Mary bundled Letty in blankets while I filled a basket with cornbread, a bit of cheese, and dried plums and threw a blanket over my head. We left our house in New Madrid, for who knew how long?

A thousand or more people, all milling about and talking at once, had gathered on Tywappity Hill, presenting a clutter of tents, makeshift shelters, and animals. We were invited to share a lean-to of wooden planks propped against a wagon, and we sat down inside it on the cold ground—ground that still shook at times. After resting a bit, I left Aunt Mary and Letty in the shelter to talk with some of the townspeople. We were all in agreement on one thing: fear haunted everyone. Fear, questions, cold, hunger, and hopelessness inhabited every sentence, strained every face.

I was surprised to see Running Wolf some distance off in the crowd, but even more surprised to see Solomon behind him. Weighted down with armloads of firewood, both appeared to be drooping with fatigue. But then everyone was tired and frightened and in a most excitable state. I had started toward them when they were approached by a tiny woman who began conversing animatedly as if they were old friends. Something seemed familiar about this woman, but I could not see her face.

Perhaps I had seen her in town sometime? Peculiar, but the way her head nodded reminded me of my mother. She was clad in a full-skirted dress with a tight bodice, a short cape, and a straw bonnet decorated with blue ribbons. Fancy clothing indeed, more suitable for spring than winter.

I heard her tell Running Wolf something about waterfalls on the river. I couldn't hear clearly, but there were no falls on the Mississippi that I knew about. Curiosity compelled me to move closer and listen without being noticed. I turned slightly, as if I were looking for someone. I heard her say she just got off a boat down at St. John's Bayou. So. It **was** the Mississippi! I listened intently. What was it in her voice that seemed familiar?

"We sped over the falls so fast," she said. "We nearly hit the boat in front of us. But it hit a floating tree, and . . ." she threw her arms into the air dramatically. "It exploded into pieces! Oh, Lordy what a sight! The crew was dumped in the water and oh, they fought for their lives, I tell you, splashing and scrambling, but they just bumped down the rocky falls anyway. I watched those men go under, then up, then down again. Our captain tried to rescue them, but he had no control of his flatboat, and both men disappeared. Such a pity." Her voice caught, and she dabbed at her eyes with a handkerchief.

Light snow began falling, and this woman opened a ruffled parasol, of all things, and continued. "Then we saw the trees waving and falling, and we knew there was another earthquake. Oh, so distressing! But the worst thing happened next, I tell you." She talked still louder, jabbing her parasol up and down as she spoke. "The river ran backwards!" She began twirling her parasol, faster and faster. "Yes it did, and then our boat went back the way we had come until it was caught in a whirlpool. We went round and round and could go neither upstream nor downstream for such a long time. Oh, what a fright we had!" Her speech slowed; her shoulders slumped. "And now I am here in this wild forgotten place, with these people." Her parasol swung in a wide arc indicating the crowd of refugees.

"And I must get to New Orleans!" she continued. "Can you find me passage?"

Running Wolf made comments I could not hear.

The wind had picked up, and although it was just after midday, it seemed colder than this morning. I shivered and shook, inside and out, and hurried back to the lean-to where Aunt Mary was huddled. She was holding Letty, who was wrapped snugly inside her blanket sound asleep. I sat down and wrapped up in my quilt. I couldn't begin to think about the next hour, the next day, or month or year. Despair swept over me, unbidden. Tears filled my eyes, but I swallowed hard and shook my head so they wouldn't spill out for Aunt Mary to see.

People came by asking about lost children, dogs, or horses. Some just stood around looking stunned. A few campfires were lit as twilight fell, and crowds moved in close to warm their fingers and share their tales of sorrow. The smell of cooking meat came in tantalizing waves on the wind.

"Missus Cummings!" someone called. Aunt Mary's head was nodding and she was nearly asleep, but I heard it clearly. "Missus Cummings!" Louder this time. "A man wants Mrs. Cummings. Anyone seen her?"

I stood and said, "Here! She's here. Who wants her?"

"That man over there." The speaker pointed to—No! It couldn't be!

"Uncle Silas!" I gasped. "Over here!"

It truly was Uncle Silas, who, upon seeing me, limped stiffly in our direction. "Whar is Missus Cum . . . Oh, there you are." He looked down at Aunt Mary, and without hesitating, snatched Letty out of her arms. "I'll be going now," he said. "Cain't git along without my child."

At that, he disappeared into the crowd, before Aunt Mary was fully awake.

* * *

CHAPTER 11

FEBRUARY 1812

Aunt Mary and I screamed, cried, ran, bumped into people, tripped over bundles and dogs. We slipped down in the slushy mud, but got up and kept going.

"Letty! My baby! Stop!" Aunt Mary struggled through the crowd. Her hands grasped air as she ran after Uncle Silas. "Stop that man!" She grabbed a stranger by the shoulders, pushing him ahead of her. "He has my baby! Help me!"

I was behind her, trying to get around and through the crowd that had gathered, blocking our way. I didn't know whether to run after Uncle Silas and ask him to come back with Letty or stay with Aunt Mary, who had slowed. Her whole body was lurching forward, grasping at . . . nothing. She fell. She gagged and vomited, whimpering between screams, "My baby. My poor baby." People backed away from her.

Why had this come to pass? Where had Uncle Silas gone? What would he do with Letty? He was nowhere to be seen. I leaned over Aunt Mary and pulled her to a sitting position. I used my shawl to wipe her mouth. We were both crying now.

She leaned her head on my shoulder, and great sobs shook her body. "My baby. He took my baby. Why?' Wet and cold and despair descended upon us both.

Someone brought warm water to wash her hands and face.

Elder Jamison appeared, and he urged Aunt Mary to get up and walk back to the shelter.

Running Wolf offered a blanket, and I tucked it around her.

The woman who had been talking to him came and knelt before Aunt Mary, whispering loudly that she should take a little whiskey to calm her nerves. Aunt Mary, upon hearing this, looked at the woman and suddenly placed both hands on her face, turning it toward the firelight.

"Pearly!" Aunt Mary said. "Are you my sister, Pearl?" She dropped her hands and sat back, squinting her eyes. "Are you Pearly? Are you? Say it is you! You were dead, Pearl! But here you are! I am Mary! Your very own sister!"

This was a dream, I thought, and soon I would awaken. This was Pearl? Pearly Everlasting, my mother? But she was dead! I saw her slip off the boat into the Ohio River last summer. I watched her bob along in the current and disappear under the water.

A dream-like unreality clouded my thinking. It was tinged with unbelievable hope, yet pierced with the same pang of loss I had lived with so long. I stared at this tiny woman, and slowly recognition of her brown eyes, the tilt of her nose, even the mole on her cheek blended into undeniable truth. My mother was alive and here, right in front of me!

"Mother?" I said timidly. "Are you truly my mother? Where have you been? I thought you drowned! Mother!

Mother!" I said again, louder, in disbelief. I wrapped my arms around her. She stiffened to adjust her bonnet.

"So it's Tansy, is it? Where are the boys, girl?"

I dropped my hold on her, for she had turned toward her sister without waiting for an answer.

"Mary. My sister Mary," she said flatly, then turned to me. "And Tansy, too. I declare, girl, you're bigger now, ain't you?"

We all struggled to our feet, holding onto one another, and looking deeply into each other's face. Aunt Mary's hands and dress were brown with mud. My mother's cheeks were streaked from Aunt Mary's hands. I, too, was dirty, but my thoughts were flittering about, trying to make sense of what was happening.

Snow began to fall, softening the moment and the utter improbable turn of events. As if from a far distance, I heard crooning words such as "sister Pearly" and " . . . back from the dead." The two women embraced, backed off, and then embraced again. I stood behind them waiting my turn. When it finally came, there was no embrace for me. My mother was busy fussing with her umbrella, trying to open it.

Snowflakes lit on my eyelashes, and I began to shiver. Aunt Mary had resumed running after Uncle Silas, calling for Pearly and me to join in the pursuit for Baby Letty. The ache in my heart all these months since losing my mother returned like a roaring beast. Mother was still the same. There was no relief at her resurrection.

"The boys are dead, Mama. Come. We must find Aunt Mary's baby."

We returned from Tywappity Hill after two days in the cold and muck. Home, such as it was, I should say. I had begun to feel at ease here in Missouri, but now I knew I would never call this home. It was a place where we existed until . . . . What? What could possibly lie ahead? Where was Uncle Silas?

My mother came home with us. She sometimes spoke of sensible things, but other times no one could understand her at all. We finally learned that she had been working in a saloon made from a beached flatboat up north where the Ohio meets the Mississippi.

"Many boats going down the river stop at our saloon there. Oh, it's such a place! I wear pretty clothes," she said, rolling her eyes back and forth. "Flounces and ribbons. And oh, the dandies, don't they like me? I dance with them and sell them liquor, and . . ."

I didn't understand what she was talking about. This was like a dream.

"Only bad thing were the rats," she said with finality. She took a quick breath. "A fine ratter we had there. Worked in that saloon too. Boy name of Solomon. I saw him in these parts, up on that hill. Might you know of him?

"Yes, Mother, I know him."

"He got rid of those varmints fast, he did. He killed the ones that lived in the hold under the deck. Sometimes ten or more in a day!" She gazed off into a faraway scene. "But he left, and then the rats got so bad." She stood and twirled around, stepping lightly, then sat back down. Her face changed again, from dreamy to determined-looking. "Going to move on to New Orleans now. They're wanting dancing girls down there."

I could hardly follow what she was saying. Solomon did seem to know her, though. He came visiting now and then, bringing us fish or turkey, or squirrels. When he and my mother talked together, I was at a loss to understand them. Actually, they didn't even understand each other, it seemed to me.

"Rats nice," Solomon would say. "Keep head warm."

"The fire is low, Solomon. Go get more rats," my mother would reply.

Sometimes Running Wolf came with Solomon. He had known both Pearly and Solomon. At the saloon, I supposed. In between conversations about pirates, evangelists, drifters, exiles, and adventurers, I came to understand that my real mother was truly gone. The woman here was an entirely different Pearly Everlasting. Only once did she look at me closely, and not look past me. She smiled then and said, "Not too plain," before she looked away.

She and Aunt Mary made sense talking about their girlhood in Pennsylvania, but recent events seemed hazy and overshadowed by Pearly's desire to get passage to New Orleans. This Pearly was on her way and had little awareness or concern for our predicament here. She never mentioned Baby Letty, not even once. Even my brothers seemed to have left her mind completely.

"The boys were drowned, Mama. We buried them in Ohio," I told her.

"Many boys in New Orleans, girl," she said.

Passage to points south had been sparse. Not many boats were able to make it down the river since the quakes. Islands had disappeared, and new ones had been created; the river had changed its course, and even experienced river pilots were not sure where the submerged trees and rocks were. Some boats had sunk after hitting underwater snags that gouged fatal holes in them. We heard about lost lives every day.

The river stopped going backward after a while by creating a new channel and several lakes. Running Wolf told us about these changes. With muddy banks falling into it, and the graveyard washing away, coffins and their gory contents clogged the channel. Trees, broken boats, and other rubble, had slowed river traffic considerably. The river had crept into New Madrid and taken some homes along the riverfront. Mistress Wilson's house was gone, as were three other houses on her lane. She had left town, I heard, and was making her way to St. Charles where she had some relatives.

Our house was still standing, although it shook badly with every tremor. Elder Jamison had again put up a sort of chimney for us, so we could build a fire. He was staying with us now, up in the loft, since a falling tree had crushed his house. Rufus had been missing since the last big quake. The reverend was quite distraught, for his dog had been his sole companion.

He told us over and over to look to God. We did pray—that Uncle Silas would bring Letty home, that the earthquakes would stop so people could rebuild their houses. But Letty was not here, and houses were destroyed. Many folks had left New Madrid, saying they would never return.

One day followed another. Hopelessness surrounded us like the winter fog. The weather was miserable, too. Rain and snow made the lanes slushy and blew into the house making us all damp and short-tempered. It was hard to keep the fire going with the wood always wet. Aunt Mary was coughing hard again. Pearly went to the waterfront every day to see about passage on some ship. She always returned, sad, chilled, and unable to talk about much of anything but getting a ride south. Sometimes she talked about the rivermen and how much they liked her dancing.

I brought up the subject of Thomas and Obadiah again, but Mama said nothing about her two sons. Aunt

Mary cried for Letty every day, but Pearly seemed not to feel, or even know her sorrow. All these loose ends were like my unraveling shawl. When a stitch broke, only holes were left, strung together.

I must be Poison Girl, just like Uncle Silas said, I thought. When I crawled into bed at night, pictures would swirl before me: Letty, my brothers, Solomon, my mother as she was, as she is now, Uncle Silas, Elder Jamison, Aunt Mary, Running Wolf. I'd lie awake trying to make sense of these whirlpool scenes. Like following a recipe for cornbread, but not having the right ingredients, there was never a finish, just a continual mixing.

Each morning I faced the day with resolve: today I would make a plan. A plan for the next week, or month, or year. But by the time I went to bed, everything had unraveled.

Sometimes when I was very busy, I would forget the swirlings for a while. But they returned, oh yes, they returned. It was like reading a book, where each page was the same as the last.

Days repeated themselves: boiling water for coffee, making porridge, hauling in wood, washing clothes. Evenings, if I wasn't too tired, I would pick up my sampler. The alphabet was finished, and I had started to embroider the verse using shiny blue silk thread for the cross-stitch words. So far it said, "Be ye ki . . . ." I needed to ask the parson the rest of the verse, so I could finish it. He would know and be glad to tell me.

He was the only one who maintained an optimistic demeanor. It was surely welcome, for it helped us carry out the daily chores that kept us alive through the fog of despair in this house.

Today I walked down to the harbor to see if Pearly had booked passage, for she had been gone a long time. Behind me I heard Elder Jamison calling out.

"Miss Tansy, do wait." He hurried to catch up with me. "Perchance I may accompany you on your constitutional today?"

"By all means, Reverend," I answered, but couldn't think what else to say. I wished I could add something, for the silence between us made me quite uncomfortable.

"Your Aunt, Mrs. Cummings, seems quite despondent, do you not agree, Miss Tansy?"

"Oh yes, sir. Indeed, sir." Now what should I say? Suddenly, here in the brisk winter air, with all the open space about us, I felt shy and self-conscious. I hastened my step, but he hurried to keep up.

"I say, Miss Tansy. That is, may I call you Tansy? You may indeed call me Uriah. Yes, please do. Uriah. That is, I see that your house needs repair, and my house is destroyed, and . . . . Oh, do stop a moment, won't you?"

I slowed my steps. He removed his hat, rolling it round and round in both hands, then looked down at me. "I say, Miss Tansy, er Tansy, I would be honored to be the man of the house. That is, if you would permit me the honor, that is, the privilege . . . that is, if you would consent to become Mrs. Jamison." He finished hurriedly, blushing brilliantly.

Squinting up at him against the winter sun, an end to the swirlings seemed possible. The weight on my heart lifted ever so slightly. I looked again at Elder Jamison and started to speak, but then an invisible curtain floated down over that momentary lightness. I wanted to answer, for the silence loomed like an intruder.

Finally I spoke haltingly. "Indeed, Sir, I do thank you for your kind offer, but . . ." I stumbled over my next words. "I must, uh, take some time to er, ponder such uh, uh, a decision." At this, I turned and ran down the path toward the harbor. I saw my mother trudging up the hill.

The next morning, I awakened to the sound of wood being chopped. It must be Elder Jamison. How good he has been to us, I thought sleepily. I turned over and stretched, yawning loudly. How pleasant to have fallen asleep contemplating a conclusion to so many problems. My mother, Pearly Everlasting, had finally booked passage on a steamship, of all things, that wonderful new invention. It would take only a few days to get to New Orleans, although it was not due to leave until March. Aunt Mary was feeling somewhat better, too, and a warm spell had arrived. A feeling of spring gladdened my heart, though warm days were still far off.

I heard Elder Jamison talking to Mr. Joe who was chattering in the persimmon tree. I wondered what they were saying. Should I marry Uriah? I rolled over and thought about being a bride. Could I wear Aunt Mary's blue velvet redingote for my wedding? I shivered with pleasure until I thought about Letty. But then again, maybe if I married Elder . . . if I married Uriah—oh, could I ever call him Uriah? Well, maybe we could go find her—together. But maybe I shouldn't marry him. What about Aunt Mary? Oh pshaw! Enough thinking for now, Tansy.

I sat up, stretched, and yawned again. My foot reached out for my kid house slipper when thump! A shock, the hardest yet, jolted the house. It shuddered, shook, and trembled more than ever before. A ceiling timber groaned and came crashing down on my leg. Fiery pain blinded me, and nausea swept me into unconsciousness.

I awakened some time later, I don't know how long it had been. Pain was stabbing my leg in knifing jabs. But what was this? I was in my bed. Beside me was a pan of biscuits and a jug of water. My leg had been bound together with the broom handle, and the house was silent. And over there, across the room, I could see the timber that fell on me!

I cried out, "Aunt Mary! Mother! Elder Jamison!" But no one answered. I called again and again. With each movement, pain racked my whole body. Slowly, the truth dawned on me: I was all alone.

*   *   *

CHAPTER 12

FEBRUARY 7TH, 1812

"Alone. Alone!" I screamed out, "I'm alone!" Great sobs erupted from deep inside of me, shuddering my whole body. With each shudder, my leg moved, and intense pain engulfed me such as I had never known. Like a Missouri mist moving in from the river, clouds of despair overtook me.

"Why? Oh, why have you left me?" I searched for an answer, but only the swish of wind in the trees could I hear, echoing the hollow emptiness of the house. Closing my eyes tightly, I went over and over what had happened: there had been another earthquake—the third big one. It seemed to be the worst ever, though the house was still standing. I had been just waking. That large timber—over there on the floor—had come crashing down onto my leg, breaking it, I was sure. It was hurting so badly, and swollen, lumpy, blue, and grotesquely bent.

And barley. All over the house was barley. I guessed the earthquake had caused that sack to fall from the loft where it was stored. Looking upward, I could see where that devil timber used to be. And there! Daylight was showing through a hole in the roof. I could see gray clouds were drifting beyond a branch of the persimmon tree.

Waves of desolation swept over me again. Whatever should I do? I could do nothing. Maybe someone would come back for me. Eagerness filled me with hope. I rolled my head back and forth, wiping tears onto the pillow, but the motion stabbed my leg again. The truth of my helplessness settled into reality, and I shouted, "Mother! Pearly! Pearly Everlasting! Come back!" But only silence and the wind in the trees answered me.

Anger came next. I felt so angry! Who would be so cruel as to leave me all alone? Mother? I didn't believe Aunt Mary would leave me—not without a plan to come back for me. But this was a very bad quake. Maybe everyone just ran. Uriah? I had been dreaming about being his wife. Did he run from the earthquake and from me? Did he hurry Mother and Aunt Mary away from here? Who wrapped my leg and put me in bed?

"I hate you!" I shouted. "I hate you for leaving me! And I hurt so much . . . ." At this, I cried again, deep sobbing wails. Of pain. Of anger. Of despair. Oh, how I hated those people, this life, this day, Missouri!

"I want my old life back!" I shouted to the hole in the roof. "With Obadiah and Thomas, and my mother and Papa!" I turned over, tears soaking the quilt, my leg hot and throbbing.

Sleep overtook me for I don't know how long. I awoke stiff and feverish. A scratching sound caught my attention. Oh, no! A rat! It was eating the barley on the floor.

"Shoo!" I yelled, throwing a biscuit at it, but it looked up at me only a moment, then returned to its meal. My leg had swollen over the top of the binding, My ankle and toes were puffed up like risen bread dough.

Later, the house shuddered with a mild tremble, jarring my leg again and causing pains, like knife stabbings. The room had darkened some, and soon night would fall. How strangely the day had vanished—in an instant, yet an eternity.

I heard footsteps. My heart leapt with eagerness. Solomon entered, walking right through the space where the fireplace had been.

"Solomon! Oh, I'm so glad to see you! Please, can you help me?"

"Please, can you help me?" he repeated.

"Solomon, you must help me. Where is my family? Have you seen Mrs. Cummings? Or Elder Jamison?" Questions tumbled out, one on top of the other. Solomon stared blankly at me, repeating the questions and smiling sweetly.

"Nice white lady sleep. Good-bye." Solomon grabbed the biscuit I had thrown at the rat and stuffed it into his hat. Climbing over the clutter on the floor, he departed the way he came in, through the fireplace.

"Solomon!" I shouted. "Don't go!"

He stopped outside for a moment and looked back over his shoulder, smiling broadly. "Good-bye, Lady." He was gone.

Night was black and frightening. I heard the rat again, maybe more than one, crunching, scratching. Occasionally there was an excited squeak. I was frightened of rats, for I saw one devour a newborn piglet once. Would it come closer and eat my toes?

Wind whistled through treetops, more vigorously than before. I thought about Uncle Silas and his superstitions. The night noises brought ghosts to mind, for I knew Uncle Silas would say they were nearby. A light rain started, then turned to snow and came softly through the broken shingles. I moved nearer to the wall to keep from getting wet. Pain was constant, and when I moved, nausea swept through me. I drank some of the water, but vomited it onto the floor.

My bladder was full, but when I tried to get out of bed I could not stand the pain. I held back as long as I could, but finally gave way and wet myself. The shameful yet comforting warmth created such turmoil in my mind, I sought escape in sleep.

But sleep came and went. Hours came and went. Darkness and light came and went. One day passed, I thought, maybe two. Time lost its daily rhythm for me. I began to believe I might die. I had hoped Solomon would send help, but no one had come. No one would come. Ever.

How long had I been in this bed? I tried to get up, but each time I stopped trying. I could not help myself. I knew if no one came to help me, I would die, alone, in this bed, in Missouri. I remembered a song Mama and the boys and I used to sing:

> *I'm just a poor wayfarin' stranger, a-travelin' through this world of woe.*
> *But there's no sorrow, toil, nor danger in that bright land to which I go.*
> *I'm goin' there to see my father. I'm goin' there no more to roam.*
> *I'm just a goin' over Jordan. I'm only goin' over home.*

I sang and said those last words again: *I'm only goin' over home . . . over home . . . over home. I'm only goin' over home . . . .*

* * *

CHAPTER 13

FEBRUARY 8TH & 9TH, 1812

I was wrung out from crying. Dullness flattened my feelings, leaving my face stiff and expressionless. Only the sometimes shaking of the house renewed my hope, for it sounded like footsteps. But it was just more quaking. Or the rat. The rat was my only company. He disappeared for a while, then returned and nibbled at the spilled barley. He carried off a biscuit, and he had eaten part of another left in the pan right beside me. His droppings were in and around the pan. Had the rat crawled over me while I was asleep? The thought made me cringe inside.

I had eaten part of one biscuit. That is, I ate part before the rat started in on it. Anyway, I was not hungry. I sipped water at times, but I thought since I was probably going to die, I might as well hasten the process. I took water only to wet my mouth. Good enough for a poison girl.

The binding on my leg was so tight, I unwrapped it. Was it yesterday? It was dark then, and now it was light. What day was it? Friday? No, it was Friday when that terrible, worst quake shook the timber down on my leg. I remember I had been dreaming about Uriah, that is, Elder Jamison, asking me to marry him. It seemed so—so nice, then. But not now! For where was he? How could he have abandoned me?

What day was this? Saturday? Or could it be Sunday? Oh yes, Saturday I changed out of my wet shift and bedding. I remember dragging myself out of bed, and with the broomstick keeping my leg straight, I used my apron under my ankle like a sling. That way I could move about, although it was awkward and painful. I finally managed to use the chamber pot. I kept fainting from pain. Twice I woke up on the floor. When I struggled back into bed, I pulled Letty's quilt up over my shoulders. It was too short, and my feet stuck out in the cold air, but I was dry.

So today was Sunday! Pshaw! A good day to die, for maybe I'd go to heaven, and see my pa and Thomas and Obadiah. Just thinking about heaven and Sunday gave me pause. I hadn't prayed much. Seemed like after bad things happened, like my mother and brothers being swept overboard, it was too late to pray. And when good things happened, well, then I didn't even think to do it. Now another bad thing was happening and would surely end badly. Perhaps this was the right time to pray, if it wasn't too late.

"Dear God,"—the words came easily, for I knew what I needed to say—"please send someone to help me. Otherwise take me to heaven. Please. And make it today, please, for I don't want to spend a long time dying slowly. I can't walk on this leg; I can't eat, only a rat is here to talk to, and he will start eating me, I'm sure, very soon. That's all. Amen."

I opened my eyes. Two rats were creeping toward my pan of biscuits. I screamed at them, waving my arms and screeching, until I was worn out.

"Come ahead," I told them finally, dropping back onto the pillow. "Eat my food, and eat my toes. I am finished with hope. I will die soon, and then you can have all of me." My mind closed itself to any possibility of rescue, or of living. I crossed my arms on my chest, closed my eyes, and slowed my breathing, hurrying death's welcome task.

I remained thus for a very long time, until sleepiness crept over me. I shifted my position, for I was getting stiff. Opening my eyes now and then, I saw that it was still daylight.

Haven't you died yet? I asked myself. *How long will this take? Or could this be heaven?* I felt cold air. Disappointment descended upon me thick and heavy, for I knew I was still alive. *Must I go through this pain, anger, and fear again?*

"Tansy Squires! Oh Miss Tansy Squires!" I heard a man's rough voice. Was it God? Was I in heaven? "I say, Miss Squires, are you here?"

I awakened quickly, aware that a voice had called my name.

"Here!" I called weakly, for my strength had drained away from me. "I am here. Who is there?"

I heard rattling and bumping and saw the door, which had been ripped off its hinges, being picked up by two large hands and set aside. A huge man, dressed in military uniform, ducked his head under the lintel and blustered into the room, dropping a canvas pack on the floor. He rubbed his hands together and noisily stamped snow off his feet.

"Miss Tansy Squires I believe? I am Corporal Seymour Dow, at your service." He bowed grandly, sweeping his military hat nearly to the floor. "Your aunt, a fine lady she is—has sent me to find you and take her news of your condition. Do you be surviving now, lassy? Be ye in comfort?"

"I am in great pain, sir. I cannot get out of bed; neither can I eat . . . rats uh eat . . . uh wetness . . ." My thoughts jumbled in a stew of mixed-up words. "Are you true, sir? Do I dream? Are you a soldier? Or God Himself, come to take me to heaven?"

My visitor smiled at me, showing large tan teeth below a grisly mustache. "I be true, missy, but I be not God." He laughed loudly, ending with a bad coughing spell. "Not God, little lassy. I be just a soldier come to fix you some grub, then I'll be gittin' along. Be dark soon, 'deed it will." Corporal Dow coughed while he built a fire in the cold ashes and put a kettle of water on to boil.

"Whar's some meal, lassy? I be fixin' ya some porridge—put meat on yer bones." He laughed loudly at his own comments, ending with another coughing fit.

"Any coffee hereabouts? I could do fer a cup myself." He dipped some oats out of a barrel and busied himself as if he were a regular kitchen maid.

I observed him with fascination, and waves of wonder swept through my heart, forcing my thoughts first up then down. Who was this man? Why had he come? *But Tansy*, I told myself, *he has already answered both questions. Yes, but why did Aunt Mary send him here after leaving me to die? And where is Aunt Mary? And my mother?* Questions, questions, yet I couldn't put words to them. I watched him. Did this mean I would live and be rescued? I wouldn't die? Cautious joy filled my heart, crowding out some of the questions. But wait! He said he would be getting along. Would I be left here alone again? Panic descended upon me once more as Corporal Dow brought me a steaming bowl of porridge.

"Here you are, little lady. This is sure to fix what ails you." He laughed and coughed loudly, then turned his head and spat onto the floor.

The smell of hot porridge filled the air, and saliva collected in my mouth, nearly choking me. My stomach growled, loud evidence of my silent hunger. I peered into this warm bowl of—hope, of life, and a future? Melting crystals of sugar sparkled on the top, a treat I had only enjoyed on holidays in the past. The first taste burned my lips, and I dropped the spoon. Looking up into Corporal Dow's face, I responded to his pleasant look with a smile, my first in many days.

"Couldn't find no coffee, Missy, but I did find some blackened taters. Finish that porridge, then, and I'll bring you a cup 'o tater coffee and be on my way." Corporal Dow bustled about the room, stirred the fire, and brought a tin pan of warm water, setting it beside my bed. Then he disappeared into the back room. I was thankful for that, for now I could wash myself privately.

He returned in a few minutes. "Missus Cummings said to give you this here laudanum. Said it would make your pain easier." He stirred some of the powder into my water cup. "Drink up, Miss Tansy." He set the cup on the floor, close to me. I resumed eating, slowing down as I began to feel full and a bit sickly.

"Tansy. Now there's a name fer ye," Corporal Dow said. "Where'd ya git a name like Tansy? Tansy ragwort's a bad pison, you know. Seems like your ma and pa shouldn't name a tyke something that's pison, now, should they?" The corporal took my bowl back to the sugar bin while he talked. Sprinkling more sugar on the porridge, he walked heavily back and handed it to me. "Keep this here oatmeal under yer blanket, lassy, to keep the rats out of it."

"Thank you for your kindness, sir. I am most obliged. Pray tell, must you leave so soon? Will you see my Aunt Mary, sir? Is she well? Where is she and are others with her?" Questions spilled out as strength had poured in. "And as for my name, my mother loved flowers and named me for the pretty yellow tansy ragwort that grew in our field."

"Wall now, that's a right nice thing to do, if'n you don't kill no cattle. You won't kill no cows, now will ya, Tansy Ragwort?" He burst into hearty laughter, sending him into another coughing fit. Wiping his eyes on his shirt sleeve, he continued. "Thar's a pretty little gal with your aunt, who's got a flower name, too. Pearly Everlasting I calls her. Sweet thing, but senseless talkin' sometimes. Wants to git down to New Orleans, she does—jist whar I'm headin.'"

"She's my mother, sir. We thought she was dead, sliding into the Ohio River as she did. But she appeared here a while back, her mind not being quite right these days. Tell me, sir. Is she well? Has she asked about me?"

"Wall now, I'll tell ya. I'm sorta sweet on Pearly, I am. I'm thinkin' I might like to squire her around New Orleans some. Think she'd take kindly to a soldier?" He twirled his mustache, slurped some coffee, and looked thoughtfully off into the distance.

"Sir," I began. "You didn't tell me about her or about Aunt Mary . . ."

"Sure enough I didn't," he said, standing and picking up his pack. "Truth be told, Pearly's a fine lady, but just talkin' about New Orleans, nothing else. Your aunt? She's doin' poorly, and that's a fact. But there's some preacher man with her, helpin' her out, gittin' food and such. He's leadin' the pack in prayin' and carryin' on like the world's going to end—which same it might do."

The corporal clomped to the door and lifted it to one side. "I'll tell Missus Cummings you ain't dead yet!" Corporal Dow, laughing heartily again, ducked under the lintel, set the door back in place, and was gone. The sound of his cough faded away until silence returned.

"Please Sir, come back!" I cried after him. But he did not return.

Hours later, in the dark, after my tears had ebbed, I made out a spider web on the cracked window just above my bed. Its outline was faint, but the comet gave a little light. I didn't remember seeing the web before. A thought that I would be covered with spiders and webs began to weave itself into my mind, but at the same time, I took note of its beauty. I had never noticed the symmetry of a spider web before.

Another quaking rocked the house. This time I watched the web. It, too, trembled and shook, and I saw a brown spider running nervously back and forth, and round and round. Then she began wrapping up a large fly, turning it with her front legs, but she dropped it out of her reach. She retrieved it and went on with her wrapping. She was probably planning on a juicy meal. I thought ruefully about the tenacity of the spider and about my own shaken life. Could I learn something from her? Perhaps there was a way back to life.

Morning came, and I had slept well. A scrunching outside the house alerted me. Footsteps. Now? Fear gripped me for a moment, until I thought about the spider. In spite of disruptions, she kept on with her plan. I, too, could keep the hope that was kindled from

Corporal Dow's visit. I would not lose hope this time. I wouldn't!

"Tansy dear. Are you here?" I couldn't believe my ears! It was Aunt Mary's voice; Aunt Mary come home to me at last.

"Aunt Mary! Aunt Mary! Is it truly yourself come back?" I twisted in my bed to look toward the door that was being pushed aside noisily. My Aunt Mary, leaning heavily on Elder Jamison's arm, entered slowly.

"Oh Tansy, my dear Tansy. You are still alive." Her voice sounded tired and weak.

The reverend ushered her into the room and sat her clumsily in the rocking chair. He straightened her bonnet that had been knocked over one eye, and then removed his own hat. He looked around the room, purposely avoiding my eyes, I thought.

Hope surged into my being like the dogwoods of spring bursting into bloom. The moment was overwhelming. Tears filled my eyes; my breath came in shallow spurts. "Oh, Aunt Mary, you didn't leave me here alone to die, did you? Thank you for coming back home." The gloomy pictures I had lived with these past hours began to assume new shapes and colors. "And my mother? Did she get passage to New Orleans?" I dared not ask about Baby Letty just yet.

"Your mother was content to stay, keeping company with the soldiers and Indians, I'm afraid." Aunt Mary tipped her head up and sniffed loudly. "We advised her to join us, but she would not."

Just then the house rumbled and shook, but this time we hardly noticed.

"And I've had not a minute's peace since we left here, my dear Tansy." Aunt Mary wiped her eyes and leaned back in the chair. "Demon Guilt has followed me every minute, plagued every thought. If we had found you lifeless, I declare I should never have forgiven myself." She sighed loudly and covered her face with her hands. "Were it not for the kindness of this good man," she nodded toward Elder Jamison, "I should have died of grief. First my baby was ripped from my arms. Then, if you . . . ." She shook her head back and forth.

"That timber, "she pointed at the offending log, "it fell on you just as the worst-ever earthquake began. Oh Tansy, I was so torn. I wanted to stay with you and care for you, but . . . the trembling of the house, the smell of the spouting black stuff, the falling trees . . ." She glanced at the reverend, who looked quickly away. "We had to run for our lives! I couldn't think what else to do. The house rattled and leaned so far that way . . ." She pointed toward the door.

Shaking her head sadly, she continued. "Well, Elder Jamison, he lifted the timber off of you. We both put you back in bed. How your leg was bent! We straightened it and wrapped it the best we could. Oh, you were groaning so, but we were in such a hurry, too . . . . Well, I put a pan of biscuits near you, dear, and the parson brought you some water. Then he steered me outside and away." She sat forward, looking serious. "And we joined the throng leaving town. I tell you truly, it was only at his insistence that we departed this dangerous house and ran for safety." She drew a deep breath and stopped talking again, her head drooping on her chest. Quiet sighs interrupted the silence.

All this time Elder Jamison was nodding agreement, a frozen half-smile on his face.

"Aunt Mary," I said softly, "did you forget about me being here alone and helpless?"

"Nay, my dear. How could I forget my own sister's child?" Tears filled her eyes once more. "I urged the reverend to come back for you, but many people up on the Hill needed him he said, and he could not leave for their pleading."

Silence crowded out further conversation. I dared not speak of my anger or my hurt. Aunt Mary, tears rolling down her cheeks, rocked her head back and forth, back and forth.

* * *

CHAPTER 14

FEBRUARY 10-14, 1812

It felt so good to be clean. I had been given food, dry clothing and a quilt. Elder Jamison brought water and soap for me to wash myself. He even took care of my wet clothes and bedding, and said not a word. Nor did I. He was quiet . . . and efficient the next two or three hours, cleaning up the spilled barley and rat droppings, setting things aright that had fallen or broken. He had gathered some persimmons from under the tree and cooked some into a hot pudding that tasted delicious. He swept the floor, helped Aunt Mary into bed, and kept the fire going. Now, as he rocked, his eyes drooped.

Neither of us spoke for some time. I was still fuzzy-headed from the laudanum Corporal Dow had given me, and I had mixed feelings today. I felt so betrayed. After all, Elder Jamison not only left me here alone with a broken leg, someone he had asked to marry, but he'd also insisted Aunt Mary leave the house. My anger began boiling over whenever I thought about it, and at times I wanted to scratch his eyes out.

But still, since coming back, he had been very good to Aunt Mary and to me. I admired him for that. But I wanted to hate him—forever. Yet I admitted, as I watched him trying to stay awake, I felt some kind of thankfulness. Perhaps because I was stronger since eating, and more content since Aunt Mary had come home.

But poor Aunt Mary. She was not very well again. She seemed weaker and thinner now, and I believed she was fading some. What would that mean?

And then there was my mother to think about. Why didn't she return from Tywappity Hill?

But back to Elder Jamison, er Uriah. He was kind and helpful, and he had a nice smile—and very good manners! Yet I couldn't help what I felt toward that man—rage toward that man of God!

Well, he did tell me the word I needed to embroider on my sampler. It should say, "Be ye kind, one to another, tender-hearted, *forgiving* one another."

Well! I didn't want to forgive him. Or Uncle Silas either. I'd rather it said, " . . . tender-hearted, *forsaking* one another." That seemed more appropriate!

The earth rumbled again. Pain shot up my leg; the web wobbled, sending the spider scurrying back and forth. Flickering firelight threw shards of light on the walls. I began a difficult prayer of thanks for my rescue, but I fell asleep with it unfinished.

The next morning was bright and sunny. Through the broken fireplace, I could see sparkling frost outside. A warm room greeted me today, as did the delicious smell of bacon cooking. I turned over in bed. It hurt my leg, but there seemed to be a bit less pain today. The thought that I was healing was so welcome. I smiled and yawned.

"I see you are awake, Miss Tansy. Will you partake of some victuals this fine morning? I have prepared bacon and scrapple, and I have recovered some genuine coffee beans from the rubble of my destroyed abode. As a result, I have some freshly brewed for you and Mrs. Cummings." Elder Jamison had a flour sack tied about his waist and was holding a steaming cup toward me.

I sat up in the bed, using both hands to lift my broken leg out onto the floor. I was careful to cover my bare leg, for I knew it would be improper for a gentleman to see it. "Thank you, Sir," I told him, reaching for the coffee.

He gave it to me, turning his eyes away quickly. "I have taken the liberty," he said, "of sweetening your coffee with a small quantity of sugar, the primary intent being to rebuild your strength after these past days of privation. I trust you will find it agreeable? A pot of scrapple is cooling and will be ready for your consumption presently."

"Thank you kindly," I said. Tasting the hot drink sent a sense of well-being flooding through me. I glanced up at Elder Jamison. He was looking down at me, a half-smile twitching the side of his mouth. At that moment I felt a glorious joy: joy at being warm and fed, joy that Aunt Mary had come home, joy at being rescued, but a strange persistent, yet unwelcome joy when I looked at Uriah. *Yes, Uriah. I think I could call him that—sometimes. For he is somewhat like a brother,* I explained to myself.

"Miss Tansy," he interrupted my thoughts, then sat down and folded his hands. "Miss Tansy, that is, my dear, I quite wish . . ." he stammered and paused.

I couldn't believe what I just heard. Did he truly say "my dear?" Is he still thinking . . . ?

"That is," he continued, "I believe I had presented you a question, that is, before the tragedy of recent days, a question regarding m-m-marriage between you and myself." He hurried through the next words so fast I barely understood them. "I quite wish to take you as a bride, my dear. Do you find it in your heart to proceed with a nuptial agreement between, uh, us?" His head tipped sideways, a look of boyish pleading on his face.

"Why, I, I don't know what to say, Elder Jamison. I truly do not know my own heart since these past days. I was so sure I would not live, and you weren't here when I needed help so badly, and . . ." I stopped and tried to clear my thoughts. Once again they swirled through my mind. Presently, I became aware of how long I had been confined to this bed. I was desperate to get up and out of this room.

"Please, Sir, do assist me. I will go outside and think through your proposal." Although sharp pain stabbed my every movement, and I was dizzy and somewhat faint, Elder Jamison helped me to the door.

"My dear Tansy, you must be aware I do the Lord's work, wherever I am called. Would you not understand that many souls up at Tywappity Hill needed comfort and solace in those hard conditions?"

There was no answer to that, for me. I leaned against the tilting wall, standing on one foot while he carried the rocking chair outside. He helped me sit and brought me a quilt, tucking it carefully all around.

"Miss Tansy, I do believe I can be a fine husband for you, and you can be a fine wife for me." He stood tall, his slim form trembling a bit, and backed up. "I might add, there is a fond affection rising within my heart toward you." With that, he turned and ducked back into the house, stumbling over the threshold.

I was filled with wonder at being outside after so long: at the brilliant sunshine, the sparkling frost. But nagging questions and conflicting answers darted in and out of my mind, interrupting the pleasant scene. I squinted against the sun, and surveyed the damaged homes of New Madrid clearly visible up and down the lane. Sinkholes rimmed with sand or charcoal, fallen trees, pools of water, high spots, low spots, cracks in the earth—all this was terrible to behold. Only the wooden houses remained upright. Brick and stone houses had turned into piles of rubble.

I wondered about my future. My mother didn't want me; Letty was gone; Aunt Mary was sick. I was beginning to think I must make some important decisions without help from anyone. But where would I start? Should I marry Elder Jamison? He was kind, even dear, in many ways. Perhaps I would be better off with him than alone. But no! I could never, ever love him. Besides, he disgusted me. He abandoned me! But what about Aunt Mary? Uncle Silas had abandoned her! And would I ever see dear Letty again? She would be turning one year old soon. Where was she? Where was Uncle Silas? And Mother! What about her? Well, I had lost my mother, for she was hardly a mother to me anyhow. Perhaps Uncle Silas had been right: I was nothing more than tansy ragwort, a poison girl.

Aunt Mary seemed weaker each day. Her face was thin and white, and her hands hung limply when she tried sitting in the rocking chair. Today she could no longer sit up, but remained in her bed. I feared she would not live much longer, and then what would I do?

I heard her weeping at times and whimpering, "Oh Letty, my baby, oh Letty." She was eating very little, too, and spoke only rarely.

The days were getting a little longer, and Uriah was teaching me to play chess. Aunt Mary had told him to find the pieces in her old trunk. I couldn't win yet, but sometimes I took several of his pawns before he had me in checkmate. We sang together sometimes, too, before it was time to sleep. He had a nice voice and harmonized when we sang, "My True Love Has Gone to Sea." When he sang the "Baylem a ding-a-lum-a dom—o-me" part his voice went so high, it filled me with mirth. His chin went way down, and his cheeks puffed out, and we both burst out laughing. I liked those times. I liked singing with Uriah. I liked Uriah—sometimes.

But stop this, Tansy, I thought. *You don't want to like him! Still . . . .*

Uriah lit the lamps, and I had just lost tonight's chess game when we heard a ruckus outside. A voice shouted, "No! No bite!" Then we heard snarling and barking and more shouting.

Uriah got up, set the door aside, and called to his dog. "Rufus! Here, Rufus. Here, boy. Come!" Then to me he announced, "It's my dog. He's been absent since the big quake!" Uriah rushed outside and soon returned with a panting Rufus, his tongue hanging out one side of his mouth, saliva dripping onto the floor. Uriah petted the dog and scratched his ears.

"Fine dog. Fine dog," he said over and over.

Just behind them, Solomon appeared.

"Solomon!" I called. "Do come inside and sit a while. Where have you been? I haven't seen you for many days."

His buckskin shirt was torn, hands and face smeared with dirt. He still wore that peculiar hat, but thankfully with no rat this time. He looked around and sat in the rocker, first moving it away from Rufus.

"Lady here." He pointed at me. "Nice lady. Dog bad." He pulled out his shirttail, showing a shredded place. A big smile creased his dirty face. "Solomon stay here now. Sleep here. Good food, Solomon hungry." He peered toward the rafters where hams had once hung.

We didn't have much to eat now. Many of our provisions had been used up or become verminous, and without Uncle Silas to replenish supplies, they were fast disappearing.

"Solomon," I said, "we have very little food, but do eat some porridge. Elder Jamison, will you kindly prepare some for my friend?" I kept my eye on the last bit of bacon wrapped up in a cloth, ready to be put into the cellar, for I remembered when Solomon had stolen our ham. I watched him as he dipped his hand into the bowl. Much of the porridge missed his mouth and fell on his lap and the floor, but he seemed unaware.

Suddenly he dived across the room, slamming his whole body down flat, the bowl of porridge flying, the chair, still rocking, sliding against the wall. Rufus jumped up and barked. Before I could take this all in, Solomon sat up, smiling broadly, and held up a large gray rat, slightly flattened and lifeless, in both hands. He held it out, offering it to me, but I cringed backward upon my bed, cold fingers of revulsion prickling my skin. At my refusal, Solomon shrugged his shoulders, stood, and placed the rat on his hat, its tail still switching.

"Solomon catch rats. Solomon good ratter. Find more in nice lady's house. Solomon stay here now. You happy Solomon come?" Again, that huge smile.

Oh my, I thought. Solomon stay here? Perhaps that was a good idea, for we did have rats, and I hated them! I wished Solomon had a home. But here? I didn't know....

Elder Jamison picked up the bowl, brought the chair back to the middle of the room, and began cleaning up the spilled porridge with Rufus's assistance. Solomon went into the back room where Aunt Mary was sleeping.

"Solomon, please do not disturb Aunt Mary. She is very sick," I called to him.

He returned, a solemn look on his face. "I show sick lady rat. She not like rat—not move. Lady dead."

Elder Jamison hurried into her room. I held my breath, for I didn't know if I should believe Solomon. Finally, Uriah returned slowly from the back room, head down, nodding. Yes, Aunt Mary was dead.

* * *

CHAPTER 15

LATE FEBRUARY 14, 1812

My eyes were red and swollen. Dear Aunt Mary, now departed from this earth. My sorrow was so burdensome, I felt inclined to lie again upon my bed and join her in death. Where, oh where was her sweet soul now? Aunt Mary had been more mother to me than my own mother, whose whereabouts I did not know, though she was alive. Two mothers. Yet no mothers. Alas, how should I fare?

> *I'm just a poor, wayfarin' stranger*
> *A travelin' through this world of woe.*

That old song ran over and over in my head.

> *But there's no sorrow, toil, nor danger*
> *In that bright land to which I go.*

Was there a bright land? Was Aunt Mary there? I hoped so. The place over Jordan sounded good. I hummed the tune again, my voice thick and catching with sobs.

I struggled out of bed, for I'd been getting up, painful as it was, ever since Aunt Mary died. Elder Jamison had made me crutches out of tree branches, so that I could walk a few steps. I was awkward, though, and almost fell sometimes.

I hobbled into the back room, though I didn't want to go there. I had never seen a dead person up close before, and I declare, it spooked me some. Uncle Silas would sure enough believe some bad luck would come to anyone touching a dead body, but I had to attend to Aunt Mary so she could have a proper burial. I didn't really know exactly what to do. My hands shook when I stopped at her bedside.

"Solomon dig deep hole," he told me, standing in the doorway. "Solomon strong man." He tightened his fists in front of him and made a face showing his teeth. "Yahh," he bellowed. "Strong man!"

Elder Jamison called to him, and they sat down at the table to make plans for digging a grave. Since part of the cemetery and several coffins had washed into the river during one of the quakes, he promised to find a spot on high ground for Aunt Mary's resting place. Solomon smiled when he heard they were going to the graveyard. He slept there sometimes.

"Solomon stro-ong man," I heard again faintly as he left the house.

I looked at Aunt Mary's sweet face and straightened her cap. I tucked loose, gray strands of hair under it, touching her cheek, then shrinking back. It felt cold and . . . and dead! Should I snip off a lock of her hair? How could I do this? I tried to remember back in Pennsylvania, when neighbor ladies went to the house of someone who had died. They would snip off some hair, wash the body, then dress it, and make it look fine. I had heard them talk about putting some memorable item into the coffin, prior to the burial. Maybe they put flowers in the hands, and oh yes, coins on the eyes to make them stay shut. I was small then, but curious. By peeking around corners, I had watched the neighbors lay out the deceased.

What should I put inside with Aunt Mary? I pondered the matter for some minutes. Perhaps my sampler, which had been, after all, for her. It wasn't quite finished, but maybe I should let it go. Yet somehow a feeling of, I don't know, ownership maybe, surfaced, and I didn't want to think of it underground. Then I was overcome with guilt. Well, perhaps a flower. But there were none to be found in February. This was hard for me. So hard. But no one else was here to help. Everyone was gone. I tightened my shoulders and distasteful as it was, I did these things for my Aunt Mary. The whole time I was washing her, I kept repeating to myself, *I'm doing this because I love you. I love you. I love you, Aunt Mary.*

She was clad in her chemise, and it was very plain and old, but her one other dress was also plain and old. "I guess you should wear some finery, but this will have to do," I told her. My voice was flat. I limped to her trunk and took out the light blue redingote. "This will cover your dress, and you will look well in a coat." I laid it atop her, but could not put it on her. I just couldn't! So I folded the redingote, placing it back in the trunk. At the last minute, I grabbed the gold-rimmed brooch that was pinned to its collar. Aunt Mary had told me the flower inside the glass was made of her mother's braided hair. That seemed more appropriate to put in the coffin, and my conscience quieted. But my leg was hurting, and my heart was in a knot.

"Why did you die, Aunt Mary? You were like a mother to me, and now you are gone." I pinned the brooch to her dress and hobbled out of the room, plunked myself into the rocking chair, and stared helplessly out the window.

The spider was still there, I noted. She had repaired her web and was busily wrapping a dead fly round and round.

"Good for you, Mrs. Spider." I spat the words out.

Just then Mr. Southward entered, his two young boys behind him. They had built a coffin out of wooden rubble lying about town, and I had seen it waiting outside.

"How do, Miss Squires." Mr. Southward lifted his hat slightly. "Come to git the body. Is it ready for buryin'?"

I indicated the back room, but kept my eyes on the spider. I listened to the shuffling and grunting of heavy lifting, the clomp of boots, and the disappearing sounds of Aunt Mary leaving home forever.

* * *

CHAPTER 16

FEBRUARY 15, 1812

The service was right nice, but not enjoyable. The Southwards carried me with the coffin, in their wagon to the graveyard. The shawl covering my head blew off or around my face as we rumbled along the lane, exposing my tears. I had a strange feeling riding next to that big box. I could hear movement from inside, as if Aunt Mary might still be alive. I shook all over during the entire trip, and pulled my shawl tighter with each bump.

Elder Jamison read from his Bible and prayed a fine prayer. He ended it with words like, "Unto Almighty God we commend the soul of our dearly departed sister, and we commit her body to the ground: earth to earth, ashes to ashes, dust to dust, in sure and certain hope of resurrection." He sang a song about Beulah land, and it was over. I could not join in the singing, for I had to clamp my throat shut to silence my sobs.

Solomon jabbered excitedly while he and Elder Jamison pushed dirt into the hole, covering the coffin. Then they took me back home, bumping along in the wagon while a brisk afternoon breeze stirred up a dust devil in front of the procession. Everyone was quiet.

As I settled into the rocker, I heard a rattily bird call outside. It sounded like Mr. Joe. He had always made Letty laugh and clap her hands, and somehow it lightened my spirit a little to think he might be there. I hobbled outside to see. Sure enough! There he was, high up in the persimmon tree. I looked at him and mimicked his rattle, then chanted,

> *One crow anger, two crows, mirth.*
> *Three crows a wedding, four crows a birth.*
> *Five crows heaven, six crows hell,*
> *But seven is the devil's own self.*

Oh, I thought to myself. One crow and I have been angry. And Mr. Joe provides a little mirth. But three crows a wedding? Oh my. Oh my. I wrapped my shawl closely about me and grabbed my two crutches tightly. Thumping as quickly as I could, I hurried inside the house and plunked down in the rocker. I had some serious thinking to do.

* * *

CHAPTER 17

LATER

Impossible! It would be absolutely impossible to marry that man. And that was final. I could never forget that he left me alone, in that place to die. I was very sure I would have died too, if Corporal Dow had not come to my rescue.

I made my way, into the back room and sat on the stool beside Aunt Mary's trunk. Opening it, I touched her pale blue redingote and felt its lovely softness once again. I had thought to bury her in it, but it seemed too lovely to put into the dark, cold ground. Since then, I had been thinking what a beautiful bridal coat it would make, and I had let myself think wistfully about wearing it for my wedding, with a blue ribbon in my hair, and I would carry a bouquet of spring flowers. Yes, I nearly embraced that dream with my whole heart. But I had put it to rest.

"*So there! And you'd better stay put,*" I told the dream, slamming the trunk lid closed.

I had begun to see clearly just what I must do, and marrying Elder Jamison was out of the question. I shook my finger in the air, repeating each word out loud: "Out-of-the-question!"

The truth was, thoughts of Letty filled my mind constantly. My, she wouldn't be a baby any more. She'd be running around and even talking some. I could almost feel her plump softness in my arms and breathe in her sweet breath as I nuzzled her neck and cheeks. I felt a strong need to find that child. Yes! That was it! I would make her my own dear child. My mind circled that possibility a few times, and then caught hold of it tightly, as if it might escape. Instantly I knew my immediate purpose. I heard Mr. Joe up in the tree shriek his approval: "Caw! Caw! Letty girl! Now! Now!"

I smiled at the peace I felt. But an unwelcome shadow, shaped like Uncle Silas, crowded into my mind, and I nearly stopped breathing. I stiffened as that shadow crept from the top of my head, down my arms, even into my hands, making them tingly and numb. I felt the sweep of that old familiar hopelessness coming back and taking up residence. But just as quickly as it came, I shooed it away and replaced it with a picture of little laughing Letty.

"Uncle Silas," I told the shadow, "I will find Letty and make her my own child. You'll just have to let that happen—somehow, some way."

I thumped noisily into the front room on my crutches swiping at that shadow, and singing loudly to drown out the "what ifs."

It's Letty in the springtime
It's Letty in the fall.
If I can't have my Letty girl,
I'll have no gal at all.

* * *

CHAPTER 18

SUNDAY, MARCH 1, 1812

Sunday and it was snowing again. I saw it piling up on the bricks outside. A gust of wind blew snowflakes inside and onto the fire, making it sizzle. I pulled my shawl and a blanket around me, for it was cold. I was feeling better and even walking without my crutches for a few steps, but the break in my leg still hurt, and I could not stand for very long.

I wondered about this house. It belonged to Uncle Silas, but he was gone, and I didn't know if he would ever return. Elder Jamison was rebuilding his own house down the lane. Even though he stayed here nights, up in the loft, he didn't have time to repair this one. What would I do when I could walk? I knew I couldn't fix this house, nor could I live here all alone. And where was my mother? I wished she would come back so we could live here together. Would Uncle Silas return home with Letty? Oh, I so wished to see Letty again, to hold her, to see her dear smile, teach her some songs, play Pat-a-cake. How I missed her.

My thoughts halted suddenly when the door scraped open. Elder Jamison stepped in slowly and came deliberately toward me.

"Miss Tansy . . . ." he began.

I looked at him, my eyes following his leanness all the way from his boots up to his serious face.

"I even now feel impelled to resume Sabbath services, Miss Tansy. Undeviatingly," he added, standing tall and straight, as if presiding over a congregation.

"And," he continued boldly, "I have taken the liberty of inviting some of the gentle folk who have returned to New Madrid, to attend a token service here, in this house, this very day. Now." His head leaned to the side, and he looked inquiringly, hopefully, in my direction.

This suggestion surprised me, for Elder Jamison had not said anything about services since the earthquakes destroyed the little brick church. I had often heard him praying up in the loft, after he had retired, although I could not hear the words. But church? Here? In this house? Now? Why, there were only four chairs, a barrel, and a rocker to sit upon. Did he assume he had the authority to do this?

"Whatever do you mean, sir? People are coming today?" At that moment, I heard voices outside, then knocking.

Elder Jamison leaped to the door and lifted it aside. ""Blessings to ye," he said to one and then another. "Welcome to the house of the Lord, my good man. Greetings in the name of the Lord, my good woman. Do enter, sir. Welcome, dear child." Soon the room was bursting with chattering folks, some I was unacquainted with, and some neighbors I knew slightly. A few sat in chairs, others stood; two children sat on the floor near Rufus and began petting him. He growled softly, but laid his chin down and closed his eyes.

I felt a sudden warmth toward these folk, not having seen anyone for many days. All had fled their homes to the tent encampment at Tywappity Hill, where last I had spoken to some of them.

"Please join me in singing a hymn to the Lord, since it is His day," announced Elder Jamison to the crowd.

"I confess I only know one hymn, Sir. My family were not church-attenders very much you see, just at Christmas." In the midst of my astonishment, I rambled on. "Aunt Mary and Uncle Silas rarely attended your services, her just having the baby and then being sick and all . . ."

"Pray tell, what is the hymn that you know," he said, "and we all shall sing it together."

"*Hark the Herald Angels Sing*, Sir. It's about the newborn baby, Jesus. I guess you know about him, Sir?"

"Indeed I do, and it is my occupation to preach to sinners about being reconciled to God, precisely as this song proclaims. Let us sing." He began lustily, and the group of about twelve joined in.

> "*Hark the herald angels sing, 'Glory to the new-born king.'*"

I found my voice by the second line and started singing softly,

> "*Peace on earth, and mercy mild; God and sinners reconciled.*"

I hadn't sung this since I lived in Pennsylvania—ages ago. But the words came back, and I sang louder, to hear myself over Elder Jamison and the others. He sang with gusto, louder still, mouth opening wide, eyes gazing heavenward.

"Joyful all ye nations rise, Join the triumph of the skies."

By now, he started harmonizing, and I declare it sounded mighty good.

"With angelic hosts proclaim, 'Christ i-s born in Beth-le-hem.
Hark the herald angels sing, Glo-ry to the newborn king."

The crowd rallied in song, and I must say, it was a spirit lifter, just like at Christmas.

"Friends," Elder Jamison began solemnly, "I welcome you here today and commend your desire to be reconciled to God. We are gathered to continue that work and to give thanks for preservation. Very few of God's children have perished, thanks be to His Providence, except for our dear departed Mrs. Mary Cummings in whose debt I stand, giving grateful thanks for her kind generosity in offering to me, a servant of God, this very domicile as a temporary habitation these weeks past.

"Friends, many of you had strayed from the paths of our Lord, but during the throes of myriad arduous difficulties in recent months, have humbly confessed the same, and are now proceeding to walk the straight and narrow, if preserved." His volume increased. "Many have determined to reinstate the habit of church attendance." His voice softened to a whisper, and he looked directly at me. "We read, in the book of John, chapter 6, verse 37 . . ." At this, he opened his Bible to a carefully marked passage, " . . . him that cometh unto Me, I shall in no wise cast out."

"My friends," he implored, "be reconciled to God. He has not left you, but perhaps you have left him!"

His voice got louder, as he swung his Bible back and forth, his top hand riding along, pointing to the words.

The sermon continued with words that pierced my heart and words that told of God's ways of cleansing the land of sin, not the least of which were the recent terrors experienced by all. The reverend paced back and forth, stepping over outstretched legs, his eyes shining with conviction, first preaching loudly, then lowering his voice so that it was barely audible.

The children gaped at the dramatics before them. They stopped petting Rufus. I, too, gaped, having never heard a sermon like this before. I confess my thoughts had often strayed in the past when trying to attend to a sermon. But this time I listened carefully. Frankly, I had been reflecting about what is true about God ever since Aunt Mary died; and yes, even before that, when I prayed to die or be saved. Come to think of it, Corporal Dow saved my life the next day after I prayed. Could that have been an answer to prayer? Did God truly hear me, or was it just happenstance?

I commenced thinking back some, and my attention wandered through a field of thoughts, but I brought it back when Elder Jamison banged his fist down on his Bible.

"Friends! Let your yea be yea!" He drew out the last words, his voice low, like when he committed Aunt Mary to the grave. "Or turn your backs on the God who preserved you." His voice shimmied slowly to silence. In the quiet that followed, goose bumps crawled down my neck.

"Let us stand for the benediction," Elder Jamison finally said and closed his Bible. He looked toward heaven and stretched out one arm, as if in salute. "Almighty and ever-living God who hath vouchsafed to preserve us thus far, forgive our wickedness, guide us in paths of righteousness, and keep us under Thy wing, as the apple of Thine eye, in the name of Thy beloved son, Jesus Christ. Amen." Ending the prayer, he began to sing, and others joined in, standing, as he beckoned them to their feet:

> *Jesus, Lover of my soul,*
> *Let me to Thy bosom fly.*
> *While the nearer waters roll,*
> *While the tempest still is high* . . . .

The song continued, but just then Rufus set up such a howling, I could barely understand the words. I did not know this song; but I did hear the words about a haven, or heaven it must mean. Wickedness? Forgiveness? Heaven? *Be ye kind, one to another, tender-hearted, forgiving one another.* The words tumbled about. More for me to think about. I saw tears on some faces as the song ended, but the children were already talking and laughing. Another quake jolted the floor, and Rufus barked his objection.

* * *

CHAPTER 19

LATER THAT DAY

"Abner! Don't push your sister like that! And mind the dog. He's a snarly one, and could be he'd bite you!" Mrs. Lamont scolded her seven-year-old son. The Lamont family and others had lingered after the short church service. That is, all but Mr. Lamont, who stood by the door obviously ready to depart. But his wife had stopped to talk to me. I was glad, for I had spoken with nary a woman in some time.

Others gathered round, inquiring about my injury, asking me how I had fared, being left alone. Grave expressions on many faces told me there was much concern and sympathy for my plight.

"How terrible for you, my child," said one.

"However did you manage to eat? Or take care of—umm—personal—umm—needs?" whispered another.

I tried to answer every question, but when I told them, privately, that I had wet myself more than once, shocked looks and gasps were hidden by gloved hands, and more sympathetic looks and exclamations poured forth.

The menfolk had made their way to the door, but no one opened it to leave. A horse outside whinnied, and its harness jingled.

"I'm sorry I cannot offer you a midday meal," I said. I remembered when neighbors had been invited in for supper back in Pennsylvania, before my mother lost her senses and when my father was still living. "Elder Jamison has been preparing food for us both, and I declare I know not what is available, if anything."

"Well, we have beans cooking at our house, Miss Tansy," said Mrs. Lamont. "Why don't I just send Horace over home to get them? If you would care to have some beans, that is, we could all eat together. Abner," she spun her son around and gave him a push. "Go with your father and help him carry the pot of beans back here." She pulled at the strings of her bonnet and removed it. "Now, have you spoons enough for all, my dear? Where would they be?"

By this time Elder Jamison was putting plates on the table. "How very kind of you, Mrs. Lamont," he told her. "There is a sufficiency in the barrel of dried pork here to share amongst us all. Your beans will be a welcome addition to this convivial repast."

"I set a batch of biscuits this morning at my house," Mrs. deJong added. "I will have them here in a short time. The fire should be just right for baking now, so's they won't burn." She laughed heartily as she scooted out the door.

Frau Heintz mentioned a kraut and potato dish she would fetch that would go well with pork, and the Wests and Madame Maisonville hurried out the door promising to bring some contribution when they returned. I was nearly dizzy from the turnarounds of the day. They all happened so quickly, and were so unexpected, but I anticipated a pleasant meal with these neighbors. I could tell Elder Jamison also looked forward to it. He hummed as he stoked the fire, and swung a kettle of water over the flames.

Later, after a delicious and filling supper, we were treated to teacakes brought by Mrs. West, and with clotted cream that Madame Maisonville had brought to go with our coffee. We sat, long after the meal was devoured and the dishes washed, talking about the earthquakes and rumors of those who had moved on and those who were returning to New Madrid. Someone said at least two thousand or more had made camp on Tywappity Hill.

I learned that Corporal Dow, the soldier from Fort Jefferson who saved my life, had been "courting a pretty little miss who doesn't make a lick of sense," someone said. I hushed my lips about her being my mother, but I asked many questions until I learned all that was to be known of her.

"She often spoke of Pennsylvania and her sheep farm," said Mrs. deJong. "But no one could get a word from her about a family in these parts. Such a strange little woman."

"Why, I heard her tell the corporal that she danced at a saloon and served drinks to rivermen." Mrs. Lamont put in disapprovingly. "That saloon, you know," she explained, "was built out of an old keelboat right where it went aground along the shore. It was up near the Ohio, you know. That was a busy saloon, I've heard tell."

The others "tsk tsked" in shocked surprise as she went on.

"Oh, she talked with him constantly, you know. I wonder why he would be sweet on that sort of woman?"

"Didn't that funny little man Solomon, I think his name is, work as a ratter there? Oh, when he arrived in the camp, didn't he make the children scream and run away? He carried rats on his head, believe it or not. Such a character!" said Frau Heintz. "Perfectly harmless, I'm sure, but ach, so strange. And dirty!"

"Strange, yes, but made in God's image," said Elder Jamison.

Everyone quieted for several seconds.

Then I said, "Has anyone seen my Uncle Silas? Did you know he grabbed Baby Letty out of Aunt Mary's arms and made off with her? Do you know anything about him?"

"I heard California was his destination," Mr. West said.

"I saw him take the baby," Mrs. Lamont said, "and he was headed east. I, myself, think he went to Kentucky or maybe Illinois. Such a shameful deed."

"I know he was born in Kentucky," I told them. "That's where he started raising roosters—before he went to Pennsylvania and married Aunt Mary."

"Well, then," Mrs. Lamont concluded, "that must be where he is. And that poor little motherless child with him. What a dreadful life for her. My, my, my." She shook her head in dismay.

The talk went on and on. I began to grow weary and needed to lie down. I stood, and that seemed to be the signal for others to stand. Soon the house was empty of all but an agreeable memory and a dying fire. It was early, but I was tired from all the excitement, and I started for bed. It would be pleasant to remember all the conversation of the day as I awaited sleep.

Some time later, in bed, I went over every word about my mother. My very own mother, who hadn't a thought about me, her daughter! It had seemed so fine when she appeared here, after I was so sure she had drowned. Of course she hadn't drowned, but might as well have, for all the mother she's been to me. She is alive, though, and now she's something special to Corporal Dow. Well, he had told me he was going to New Orleans, and my mother was heading that way too, she said. Perhaps I would never see her again.

Though I was just fifteen, I felt like I must decide things for myself now. Like not marrying Elder Jamison and not expecting my mother to be a mother. Is this what growing up means? You lose something, but then find something different in yourself? Does it always take sorrow to understand this?

Now about Uncle Silas and Letty. I turned over in bed and pulled the quilt up over my shoulders. The room had cooled off considerably, but I wasn't sleepy. I had too many things on my mind. I needed to finish the thought I started a day or so ago, the one about making Letty my own child. Yes, that thinking was taking root. A thrill of anticipation engulfed me at the possibilities. But where would I start? How would I find her? Would Uncle Silas let me have her? Would I have to steal her from him, like he stole her from Aunt Mary? I'd heard he might be in California, or Illinois or Kentucky. Well then, I would go to all those places. I would start with Kentucky, for it is closest. Now how would I get there? Fording the river would be a problem, but I could ask the boatmen if they would ferry me across. I could take them a pudding or a cake, and I'm sure they would oblige me. Just as soon as I was walking without pain, I would start out. Yes I would!

I opened my eyes wide and sat up. Outside, the night was bright with moonlight on the snow. I was fully awake now, making real plans—plans with a future to draw me instead of bury me. Tomorrow I would tell Elder Jamison I have made up my mind and cannot marry him. Then I'll ask him to show me how to hitch Maxwell to the wagon and drive him to Aunt Mary's grave. I would tell her my plans. I believed she would feel kindly about me raising Letty. I would practice driving that mule, too, for I've never done such a thing before. But I could learn—sure enough I could learn. I'd watched others do it. And as soon as I could, I would be on my way to find my Letty girl. And then? I didn't know about that yet.

I lay down again and curled up under my quilt. Now I could sleep, for my mind was made up.

* * *

CHAPTER 20

MARCH 2-5, 1812

"You stupid mule! Get back in the lane and stop eating. Now!" Oh! I was so weary of shouting at Maxwell. After Elder Jamison had showed me how to hitch this mule to the wagon and how to drive, he went back to the house. All went well for a while. But then this obstinate beast veered into a patch of grass and wouldn't budge except when I shouted. Then he turned to look at me as if I had lost my senses. He switched his tail, tossed his ears and went back to eating. Pshaw! Pshaw! Pshaw! I almost cried. I was so angry I didn't know what to do. There I sat, stuck. For how long? It must have been almost an hour. How I wished for someone to tell me what to do. I had so many plans and so much to do, and this was only the beginning. But I couldn't do any of them if this mule wouldn't budge.

"Maxwell!" I shrieked as loudly as I could, but still he didn't move. I dropped the reins and slumped, my eyes squeezing hot tears down my cheeks.

Suddenly, I was aware of the wagon moving. Looking up, I saw Elder Jamison in front of Maxwell, his hands firmly holding each side of the bridle. He was pushing this stubborn mule backwards. And Maxwell was moving! In truth he backed right to the middle of the lane, switched his head and let out a loud, "Hee haw!"

"Oh! Elder Jamison, you frightened me. But look! You pushed Maxwell right into the lane. How did you know to do that?"

"I have had some acquaintance with mules, Miss Tansy," he told me.

"Thank you. Thank you—a thousand thanks," I said. Then I remembered my screech at Maxwell, and cringed with embarrassment. I felt my face burning, and when I looked at him, I saw that the reverend was grinning. He turned away and clapped dust off his hands.

It wasn't easy getting Maxwell to the cemetery. I just accepted that he was a stupid animal with no sense whatever. He was strong, though, and finally carried me to my destination in the wagon.

The ground was mostly covered with snow, but I could see that the grave was still barren of grass. I was pleased that spring was just around the corner, and it wouldn't be long until new sprouts appeared, and maybe even a few flowers. I hoped none of those pesky wild onions would grow on her grave. That wouldn't seem right somehow. I knelt down and told Aunt Mary of my plans. I knew she couldn't hear me, but it felt fine to pour out my heart to her.

Maxwell pulled the wagon homeward with no dawdling. My leg was smarting by the time I returned home, but I believed I could truly drive that wagon well in a week or two. I'd be loading it with oats and hay for Maxwell, some provisions for me, and of course some of Letty's things. She would have outgrown the little embroidered frock that Aunt Mary made. I knew she would be much bigger than when I'd seen her in December.

I had finally talked some courage into my mind—enough to turn down Elder Jamison, and also to tell him I was planning to leave New Madrid to search for Letty. He listened politely, saying nothing. I had thought he might try to discourage me, or repeat his proposal of marriage. Or worse, insist on coming with me. An awkward silence hung suspended above us. Then he spoke seriously:

"Allow me to assist you, Miss Tansy. I will, if you agree, accompany you across the river and see you on your way to Kentucky." He sat down at the table and leaned forward on his elbows. "Then I, too, shall part company with you, for I have felt the Lord's call to move on from here."

"What will you do, Sir? Where will you go?" I confess I felt some concern for him.

"My sister, I have learned, has moved to Natchez," he told me. "She writes of the sin of that city, as well as its horticultural wonders. She particularly lauds the magnolia trees, which will soon be in bloom. I should like to assist my dear sister in her agricultural endeavors, while plowing the fields of sin." With that, he stood to let out Rufus, who was whining at the door.

Returning to the table, we talked for some time until it was dark. I was pleased that we each had plans and would embark on journeys befitting our own desires. I must confess I was also pleased that he had dropped the subject of marriage—but a mite surprised he let it go so easily.

I practiced daily with Maxwell. He was beginning to understand me. And I was learning to speak firmly to him without screeching and make him obey. He could be lovable sometimes, but just when I'd think he was my friend, he'd turn stubborn again. I wished there was a better way to find Letty, but this was how it must be.

I returned early today from my practice trip, for it had begun to rain. The rain meant winter was departing. The air was a bit warmer, and I saw tiny buds swelling on the persimmon tree. Aunt Mary had said the fruit would be yellow-orange but not ripen until fall. I would miss them, but I was sure Mr. Joe would have a fine feast.

Rufus rode with me today, and he drooled down my neck on the way. That scamp! I was just scolding him as we arrived back home and pulled to the shed in back of the house. He jumped out and began barking, running toward the door. He barked and barked as I loosed Maxwell and swatted him into the shed. *Someone must be here*, I thought, as I set the door ajar and peered inside.

"Pearl! I mean Mother! Pearly!" I rushed inside nearly knocking her down as Rufus bumped past me to sniff this stranger. My mother was standing in the middle of the room, and who was beside her but Corporal Dow! I was stunned and knew not what to say.

"Your mother and Corporal Dow have come here to be married, Miss Tansy," said Elder Jamison. "You are just in time for the ceremony. We've been awaiting for your arrival."

I was utterly speechless. My mother looked happy and fluttery, although she said nothing. She was wearing a pretty straw bonnet with velvet flowers matching her lavender silken dress. Ribbons of yellow, lavender, and white were tied gaily under her chin.

"Greetings, little lady," Corporal Dow addressed me, bowing slightly. "I have at length asked this pretty miss to be my bride, and she has agreed. I think." He laughed loudly and slapped his knee with his hat. "Let's git on with the ceremony, Rev'rend. Forget the lines that ain't essential. We've got a boat to catch before it weighs anchor."

"Mother, are you sure you want to marry Corporal Dow?" I asked.

"I do," said my mother, looking up at her husband to be. "I sure do."

The wedding started and was finished before I could grasp the situation. "I now pronounce you man and wife," called Elder Jamison. "You may kiss the bride." The corporal pecked his wife's cheek, grabbed her hand, and the two were out the door by the time the last words were spoken.

* * *

CHAPTER 21

MARCH 16, 1812

No snow had fallen for a week. I was glad, for it would be easier traveling. I had been thinking about what it would be like to drive a mule a long distance all by myself. There were wild animals in the forests of Kentucky. And swamps and millions of mosquitoes. Elder Jamison insisted that Rufus accompany me, and I was quite glad to have that assurance. His bark scared off the possums and coons that prowled around the house at night. He would be valuable and good company on my trip.

The reverend also had been giving me further instructions about driving that stubborn mule as if he were my father. Come to think on it, he was more like a brother—a brother who cared for the welfare of his sister. Well, that was a good way for us to part.

He told me several times to inquire at any cabins along the way if I might spend the night there. I should take along hardtack and cornbread, cheese, and dried meat, and offer some to folks who would put me up. If I couldn't find a cabin, he said, I should sleep in the wagon with Rufus close by.

And, this was the part that was worrisome. He said I must take Uncle Silas's rifle. He commenced to give me lessons in shooting. Oh, what a sore shoulder I had! That rifle seemed to hold a grudge against me, for it kicked me hard with every pull of the trigger. However, I was becoming more accurate each day. My "brother" Jamison said I would be ready to leave when I had shot a rabbit, and we had eaten it in a stew.

I opened Aunt Mary's trunk again. Her beautiful redingote was right on top, for I had tried it on many times. I kept thinking I should have dressed Aunt Mary in it for her burial. She would have looked so beautiful. But something wouldn't permit me to bury that lovely coat. A strange thought crawled into my mind: How could I bury her, but not her coat?

Look not backwards, but ahead, I told myself. Ah, there was the mirror in which she had smiled at herself, and some gloves, two books, her marriage certificate—all tattered and brown around the edges. There was also a small, carved, wooden box with beautiful pearl earrings inside. Ah, what was this? Down on the bottom were several coins. I asked Elder Jamison about them, and he called them Spanish reales. They would be helpful sometime, he told me, if I were ever in trouble, and I should take them with me.

There was a sampler, too! Aunt Mary must have made it when she was a child. The words were in French, for I made out *L'amour,* but nothing else. Such pretty flowers were embroidered on it. I would take this with me; it should belong to Letty someday.

One of the books was a Bible. I opened it. The print was so tiny, I could barely read it. My mother had taught me to read from the Bible, but I'd nearly forgotten everything. I did recall some of the Psalms, though, that they were quite nice to read at times, almost like songs.

The last thing I found, next to the coins, was a pair of fancy buff-colored shoes. How pretty they were! How smooth and shiny the leather! And I was quite taken by the heel. It was not too high, and it was so, so graceful. I tried one on, for I was about the same size as Aunt Mary. It fit! I put on the other shoe and fastened the tiny buttons up the side. Then I danced around a bit, though with a limp. The shoes were wondrously fine. I decided right then to take them with me.

Indeed, I would take the whole chest with me! It would always remind me of Aunt Mary, of Missouri, and of this year of extraordinaries. And not only the terrible earthquakes, but also the year I was proposed to, the year I nearly lost my life, the year I found a new direction, and the year I decided about Letty. As I settled that question, a sense of peace descended upon me.

Today a new thought slid in silently with the others, fixing the welcome peace securely in place: I would never return to Missouri.

* * *

CHAPTER 22

MARCH 21, 1812

The first day of spring didn't feel like spring at all, for it had snowed during the night. But sunny days followed, and the snow melted. Tiny green sprouts poked out of the ground. Buds swelled larger each day on the persimmon tree.

We loaded the wagon with the last provisions while Rufus ran round and round barking at Mr. Joe perched up in the tree. Mr. Joe, I do believe, has company, for I saw another shiny black crow in an old oak across the lane. They seemed to be talking back and forth. Perhaps he was telling her to stay where she was as long as that ferocious dog was nearby. I brought out a handful of dried corn and threw some on the ground by the chopping block. Mr. Joe looked down, his wings open, ready to fly, but Rufus bounded over and ate every kernel! How that dog was scolded by Mr. Joe!

"You'll just have to learn to fend for yourself," I told him, as I heaved a roll of blankets into the wagon.

I was quite animated, even giddy, for this was the day I would leave Missouri. We had given many of the household goods and animals to neighbors who had been laboring to fix up their houses. Even though we still experienced shaking and rumblings in the earth nearly every day, they were not as frightening as they once had been. I might say we took them in our stride; they had become commonplace.

Since this house belonged to Uncle Silas, I would not let myself be troubled about it, for I would not be returning here. I was glad to leave and to start a new life.

A little thrill ran through me sometimes—a tingling, heart-pounding feeling. I knew not what to call it, but it was very real. It appeared whenever I thought about what may lie ahead. Visions of forests, animals, Uncle Silas, sweet Letty, hunting for rabbits, Rufus barking at danger—all these things paraded through my head, and then that feeling would start up. At times I questioned whether I was being foolish, and I would quake with anxious thoughts. But when I took them apart and looked them in the eye, they quivered and shrank, and the goal I'd set grew firmer and larger. I was more determined than ever to get into the thick of it. The sooner the better.

We climbed into the wagon and waved good-bye to the neighbors who had gathered to see us off. I flapped my arms at Mr. Joe, hoping he understood my attempt at crow talk. I snapped the reins on Maxwell, and we were off. That is, we would have been off, if Maxwell had moved!

"Git, Maxwell! Git up!" I told him.

"Hee haw!" he brayed, shook his long ears, and just stood there.

Elder Jamison got out and smacked his rump, shouting, "Git along, you stubborn mule!" and Maxwell finally began inching down the lane.

"Good-bye, good-bye," we called and heard, until we were out of earshot. We passed the Southwards' house, but no one was about. Then we headed over the barren rise where I first had met Solomon in the grove of trees. The earthquakes had since toppled most of them. I looked downriver to the waterfront where Mistress Wilson once lived, but the river covered the road now, and all the houses had collapsed or washed away.

Gazing downriver, I saw a keelboat tied up at St. John's Bayou, the very one that would take us across the river. Oh, there was that tingly thrill feeling again!

"Do you think the river men will agree to take us across to the other side?" I asked the reverend, as Maxwell dawdled along toward the harbor. "Can they be persuaded?"

"Indeed, yes, Miss Tansy. I have arranged with them to do so. And by offering to present them a pudding, that delectable edible will surely secure our passage." He straightened his cravat, adjusted his hat, and looked straight ahead.

He was strangely quiet today. And he was dressed like a real gentleman. I had never before seen him with a cravat, or with his pantaloons tucked neatly into his boots. How fine he looked in his long-waisted coat. I glanced sideways at him and suddenly felt plain in my faded homespun dress, which, I might add, was feeling tighter across my chest than when I arrived in Missouri. I supposed I was still growing—in body as well as mind, and I was glad for growth: for mine, for the hints of spring to come, and for the rest of my life, whatever that may be. I started to sing as we rode along:

> *My true love has gone to sea*
> *Baylem a ding a lem a dom o me . . .*

Elder Jamison joined in, but rather less robustly than at other times, it seemed to me.

Arriving at the dock, he talked with the boatmen, and gave them the pudding. They were pleased, and thanked me. They began unloading the wagon. A line of three workers and the reverend tossed parcels to one another, and finally to the captain who was on the deck. Rufus waded in and out of the water, barking and chasing birds and a family of baby ducks trailing behind their mother. He, too, seemed eager for this new adventure.

It took nearly half an hour to coax Maxwell up the catwalk. We had to unhitch the wagon, for he refused to pull it. The boatmen dragged the empty wagon on board, grunting at the effort. Then we climbed on, the captain weighed anchor, and we were on our way. The boatmen dug long poles into the shallow water, pushing the flatboat away from shore.

When we left the quiet calm of St. John's Bayou, the strong current of the Mississippi caught us, and we fairly flew down and across the river. The captain steered the boat with a tiller, he called it, a long paddle that was attached to the stern. This trip was somewhat frightening, but no one else seemed nervous except Rufus. He laid his head on Elder Jamison's knee, flattened his ears, and no longer wagged his tail. A pitiful whine stole across the deck, and I wondered who would comfort whom on this journey.

A canoe full of Indians paddled by. My heart jumped into my throat when I saw them, for I had heard they sometimes attacked boats and shot at them with bows and arrows. Thankfully, they did not seem interested in us and continued down the river. When we pulled up to the Kentucky shore, Maxwell was more eager to get off the flatboat than he had been to board it. The supplies were unloaded onto the dock, then piled back into the wagon. Maxwell was hitched up once again. When all was ready, I faced Elder Jamison to thank him and bid him good-bye.

Strangely, I felt my cheeks burning hot. I didn't know why, for he was like my elder "brother" and had been very helpful to me. Raising my gaze, I was suddenly without words. All this time he was looking down at me so kindly, so sincerely, with a slight smile. And what else did I see? Some slight moisture in his eyes. That made my cheeks burn even more, for I was aware of some strong feelings swirling through me. And I thought I sensed the same from him. This was so-so awkward.

"I do declare, Reverend, I am caught without a proper farewell." I laughed nervously and swallowed, then swallowed again. I choked and coughed and looked at him helplessly, unable to speak.

He cleared his throat and wiped his brow. "Miss Tansy," he said, "you are in Kentucky now, and it is time for you to journey onward. I shall leave you here." He shifted from one foot to the other. Maxwell snorted, trying to bite at a fly.

"May I suggest that you follow the river as it flows south?" he continued. "In a while you will find yourself in Tennessee, but fear not. The river turns east for a time, then north, and as you follow it, you will again be in Kentucky." He stopped speaking and cleared his throat again. I noticed his forehead had sprung more beads of moisture.

"One last thing, my dear Tansy." He took both my hands in his. "I—that is, you—er—that is, I shall bid you adieu now . . . ." He squeezed my hands so hard, they hurt. "That is, oh Miss Tansy, do write to me of your successes—and failures, if any. I—uh—will always think fondly of you, my dear. And if . . ." He paused, coughed, and went on, "if you should ever need my assistance, or . . ." he spoke rapidly now. "If you should reconsider my late proposal of marriage, I would be gratified to hear the same and would present myself hastily in your vicinity." He dropped my hands, reached for his kerchief, and wiped his mouth and brow.

I turned to look toward the forest, for I had not the will to think on that subject again, nor even consider this man's proposal. My firm purpose kept repeating itself over and over in my mind, with no room for other thoughts: *Find Letty. Make her your own child. Find Letty.*

Elder Jamison turned around and walked slowly back toward the boat.

The barren oaks, their branching fingers twined together, formed an arch of sorts, framing a wagon trail into the dense forest. It seemed to welcome me, and I was eager to go.

"Farewell, my friend! Farewell!" I called to him and climbed into the wagon. "Git up, Maxwell.

* * *

CHAPTER 23

MARCH 23, 24, 1812

For two days I traveled through Tennessee. The trail near the river was wide enough for my wagon, so I didn't have to struggle through the tangled underbrush. But when the trail ducked deep through the dark forest, and the river was out of sight, the trail narrowed, and oftentimes branches slapped me in the face. I found myself feeling anxious and my pleasure waning. I imagined I could see eyes shining from the shadows. Sometimes there truly were eyes. I had the rifle primed and ready, but so far the animals had stayed away. Perhaps they were as wary of me as I was of them. I hoped so.

I saw a few houses on high banks along the river. I stayed the first night with a large family in a small cabin. They provided Maxwell with fodder, and gave me fish and beans and squash to eat. Rufus found food scraps near the hog pen and had a time of it. He barked at the hogs when they grunted from behind their fence.

A hot cup of coffee was offered me, too, and was warm and pleasant after the long wagon ride. I was obliged to sleep on the floor with several children. I shared my quilt, but it was pulled off during the night, so I was cold and did not sleep well.

In the morning, I was fed again. This family had plenty of food, but only ragged clothing and few blankets. I counted six children, all very young, and I couldn't help but notice another would be added to the family soon. The man of the family, Mr. Twining, told me I'd be in Kentucky an hour hence.

Before I started out again, I inquired about Uncle Silas. "Silas Cummings," I told them. "He has a young child with him. Have you seen or heard of him?" I was so eager to find Letty, I asked everyone I met.

"Cain't say as I have, Miss. But then we ain't been here long." He headed toward the hog pen, a bucket of slops in each hand, getting on with his chores. I took my leave, waving good-bye to the children, grateful for the packet of food given me.

Most folks I'd asked gave a similar response to my inquiries. No one had seen or heard of Uncle Silas or Letty. My surprise was great when on the third day out, I stopped to inquire about lodging. During the conversation, I was told about a cockfight that was to take place that very evening. The mention of the same set my hopes soaring, for Uncle Silas might well be involved with that sickening sport in these parts. He had been breeding gamecocks for years and had often attended such competitions, leaving Aunt Mary and Letty and me at home for many days at a time. I recalled that he would set off with a wagon full of roosters he had raised to be good fighters. When he returned, he wobbled strangely and talked like his tongue was tied in a knot. Aunt Mary would purse her lips and speak very little to him for the rest of the day, although I heard the words, "demon rum" muttered under her breath a time or two.

"Where might I find the cockfight, sir?" I asked.

"Down yonder, close by the mill, young miss." He pointed back toward the woods. Then he looked at me with amusement. "You ain't plannin' on goin' to a cockfight, are ye? Ain't a fit place fer a lady. It sure ain't." He lifted his battered hat and scratched his head. Straw fell onto his shoulders.

"Yes, sir, I am. I am looking for my uncle, Silas Cummings. Might you know him, sir? He has an interest in cockfighting, and if he is nearby, I am sure he will be in attendance."

"Well now, ain't that a occasion of chance? I knows the man well, I do." He shook his head thoughtfully, loosing another shower of straw and dust. "Now if you gits there some time before sundown, you'll find that feller fixin' little knives to his roosters' feet. That's a man what has raised a dandy bunch o' fighters, 'deed he has."

"Thank you kindly, sir," I said, turning Maxwell around and heading back into the forest. I was elated and that old familiar tingly feeling started up in my breast once again. Maxwell sauntered along slowly, though I shouted at him and poked him with a long stick trying to hurry him. Would Letty be just an hour away?

After a while, by following the din of hollering and squawking, just as I was advised, I found Uncle Silas. But no Letty was in sight. As I came into a clearing, I called to him.

"Uncle Silas! Good afternoon to you." Hauling on Maxwell's reins to stop, I jumped down from the wagon and approached my uncle. "Do you fare well?" I felt I must be polite, although I had many mixed feelings about him.

He looked up at me quizzically, but then back at a struggling cock on his lap.

"Uncle Silas, it is Tansy, your own niece come to find you. And Letty," I added, holding my breath. "I trust you both are prospering and in good health?" I forced these words to come out distinctly and take shape properly, although in my thoughts I was shouting, *Where is Letty? Let me have her, and I will take her away from this place and raise her as my own child.*

"She ain't here, and you shouldn't be neither." He got up and threw the rooster over a fence into a pen, where it squawked and flapped its wings and ran round and round.

Moving to another pen, Uncle Silas chased after a large white bird until he caught it. Holding it by its feet, he put a hood over its head, and sat down on a stump. Restraining the bird between his knees and grabbing one foot, he began winding twine around a piece of leather holding a sharp blade against the rooster's leg. He adjusted its angle carefully. He seemed to want it placed just right.

"Danged bird. Hold still, you fowl critter!" He ignored me and the loud cheers coming from beyond the cages. I looked that direction and saw some hats fly high into the air. I guessed a cockfight was just ending, and I confess I was a mite curious.

But I couldn't wait to bring up the subject for which I had come all this way. "Uncle Silas, where might baby Letty be these days? I was in hopes of seeing that child again."

"Gone. She gone. Too much trouble, her screaming all the time. Got work to do, doncha know. Pert' soon got to git these cocks into the ring, yonder." He indicated the arena of sorts, with logs for seats, beyond the rooster cages. "Cain't be watchin' a fussin" child all the time. Makes the birds nervous." He continued wrapping a blade on the rooster's other leg.

He had barely looked at me, nor had he inquired about poor Aunt Mary, rest her soul. I was dismayed at his lack of concern, and unsure what to do or say next. But only for a moment. With renewed courage, I took a step closer and threw back my shoulders, disregarding the uncomfortable encounters with him in the past.

I willed my words to soften when I spoke. "Uncle Silas, I'll be glad to take care of her—I'll even raise her as my own, if you'll tell me where she is." There. I told him what I wanted. Whatever would he say about that, I wondered breathlessly, my heart pounding in my chest.

"Gave her to a Indian, I did," said Uncle Silas. "Dang! This rooster kicks hard! He's cut my hand now, goldurn bird. Jest you bein' here brings me bad luck." He threw the rooster over the fence into its pen, its squawking filling the air so that I nearly missed his next words: "Old squaw going after them pigeons what flocks to the woods purt' soon." He pointed toward the east. "Might be you could find her thereabouts. I be gittin' these birds over to the ring now, doncha know. You'd best git away, girl. The next fight's startin' soon."

At that moment, a caged rooster was carried triumphantly out of the ring, a cheering crowd following. Close behind them, a short bewhiskered man carried a limp, bloody rooster by one leg, its comb torn and wattle shredded, patches of bare skin showing. Whirling it above his head, he gave it a toss into the bushes. Rufus bounded after it; I turned my attention to Uncle Silas.

"How far away is that, sir?" I couldn't be dismissed without more information. I didn't know what he was talking about. Pigeons? Flocking to the woods?

"Can I get there before dark?" I pressed him further, wondering if I could find the place. "How do I get there, Uncle Silas?"

He acted annoyed. "Jest go, Tansy Ragwort, Poison Girl. Jest git gone from here. And take that child, should you find her. She's too much for an old man. Got to work these roosters, doncha know. Git along, now, down through the field yonder. When you come to a creek, follow it east, cross it where the trees are thickest, and you'll soon see folks gatherin'. Might be that squaw is there with the tyke. Purt' soon comes them passenger pigeons. That's what folks is a wantin'. Now you git. You hear? This ain't no place for a girl—even a poison girl. Night air's bad fer girls, doncha know." With that, he kicked over the stump he'd been sitting on and, picking up a cage with a squawking rooster inside, stomped toward the ring, dust rising in brown clouds from every step.

I got back into the wagon and called Rufus. Although I could hear cheering and squawking, I didn't stop to watch. I smacked the reins on Maxwell, and we departed through the field. It was dry, and the grass crackled as we plodded along. I followed Uncle Silas's instructions and drove along the creek for some distance. The sun was near to setting in the west when I saw the thickening forest. I crossed the creek, and sure enough, many people were gathered in a small clearing: settlers, Indians, children. Carts and wagons of all sizes were parked under trees, and everyone seemed to be standing around waiting for something.

I looked at every Indian I saw, but didn't know who I was looking for. Well, Letty was who I was looking for, but first a squaw. Yet which one? I inquired of many Indians.

"Baby? Do you have a white baby this tall?" I held my hand up showing the size I thought Letty would be by now at fourteen months old.

Some ignored me. Some said no and turned away. Some looked blank at me as if I were a simpleton. One squaw smiled a toothless smile and told me she had "many babies." She asked me how many I wanted.

Feeling panicky, I turned to ask another group. Tears made their way into my eyes and down my cheeks. Oh, I was so tired and fearful!

"Here they come!" a voice shouted. I turned toward the sound. Everyone was looking at the sky as a few birds flew overhead. Just as I was wondering what was so important about a few pigeons, a shotgun blast cut through the air. Then another and another. Suddenly the sky was black with hundreds of birds flying overhead, some landing in trees, some falling from gunshot. The noise of their wings and chatter, as well as the guns blasting all around, caused such chaos. I didn't know where to look or what to do. I felt like escaping, but Maxwell lay down, and I couldn't persuade him to get up. So I just sat there and covered my ears. Rufus cowered under the wagon seat and howled pitifully.

For several minutes I remained thus, the noise never ceasing. Twilight deepened, but birds kept coming. It seemed like an hour had passed, and still they came. Thousands by now. Dead birds littered the ground; children and women picked them up and threw them into the wagons and carts. Someone started filling my wagon.

"Stop!" I shouted. "I don't want any birds. Do you hear me? Stop!" But they didn't stop.

Many wagons full of birds began leaving the area, but many more carts and wagons arrived as guns fired and birds fell. My wagon was still being filled with dead or half-dead, wing-flapping, bloody birds. Although I was used to plucking chickens for stew, I had never seen so many fowl at one time. I became sick from the smell of gunpowder and warm blood and the sight before me. Saliva collected in my mouth, and I wiped my face on my sleeve.

An Indian family with their arms full of birds approached my wagon and dumped their load into it. "Stop!" I screamed, and grabbed handfuls of wings and feet and threw them out on the ground.

"No more! No more!" I kept shouting as I threw two and three at a time out of my wagon.

I looked at my hands. They were red with warm blood. A few feathers were stuck to them. I burst into tears. My body shook; my hands hung down in limp defeat. Rufus started to lick them, and I let him.

The Indian family backed up a few steps and watched me with solemn faces. Now I felt silly, as if I were a spectacle for their entertainment.

"You have wagon, miss. Take birds to village. You follow." The father of the group, an ear ornament shining in the dim light, gave me such a fright. He tugged on Maxwell's harness to get him up to start walking. The wife and three little boys picked up handfuls of birds, and tossed them back into the wagon, running to catch up. The girl of the family, about twelve I would guess, followed along behind. She was wrapped in a large blanket, making her appear quite stout.

Where was this family leading me? What would happen to me? Why was I following this Indian, anyway? But what else could I do? I feared I was losing my resolve, my purpose. Weariness swept over me in waves, keeping time to Maxwell's plodding steps.

* * *

CHAPTER 24

MARCH 24, 25, 1812

They led me through the dark forest for two hours or more. No one spoke. I was so tired, and these children surely grew tired too. Birds clamored in the trees above us. There must have been thousands of them, and I could still hear hundreds flying, high in the sky.

When would we arrive at their village? I sighed heavily. Just then I saw fires ahead, and the village was there, right in front of us! Perhaps I should have been afraid, but I was too tired. And hungry, too. We stopped in front of a wigwam, and the family disappeared inside. Now what? As I looked around, the father came out and handed me some dried fruit and beans in a clay bowl. He then freed Maxwell and led him to a pan of water.

"Come," he said to me, indicating the doorway. Inside, it smelled close—like soggy burned-out logs. My throat tightened and my eyes squinted trying to see in the dim room. The mother added sticks to the weak flame that quickly grew into a warm fire, lighting the arched poles and walls.

The children were lying on mats, all except the girl. She sat by the fire. A small child was sleeping on her lap. That surprised me, for I hadn't noticed any other children. I peered closely, for in the flickering firelight, it was hard to see clearly. There was something familiar about the child. I couldn't tell if it was a boy or a girl. It was wrapped in the blanket the Indian girl had been wearing. She must have been carrying this child all the way from the bird-shooting. It turned its head, and I saw that it had light hair. The others all had dark hair. A tiny thought began to grow in my mind. I leaned closer. Could this be Letty? No, it wasn't—it couldn't be. But the child's size was right, and the light-colored hair was right. Would an Indian child have light hair?

I leaned even closer. This was Letty! I was sure of it. I reached for her, but the girl turned away, pulling the child with her.

"Letty!" I said softly. The Indian girl looked up at me, fear in her eyes.

"She is my cousin," I told her. "Give her to me." I reached again, but the girl still held the child tightly, and would not let me have her.

The mother spoke a word sharply. The girl looked resentful, but loosened her grip. I reached for Letty again, and this time took her in my arms. She was heavier than I remembered. But of course! It had been nearly three months since I had seen her. She stayed asleep, her head on my shoulder, her warm body nestled limply against mine.

"Oh Letty, sweet Letty girl," I crooned. "It's Tansy, your cousin Tansy." I nuzzled her soft cheek. "I've come for you, Letty. You are my own girl now."

Around me, in the firelight, all was quiet. The boys were sleeping. The girl sat, looking gloomily into the fire. The mother, who had been watching, rocked back and forth, and started humming a sort of chant, repeating the same words over and over. It was a strange song, but somehow soothing. I swayed back and forth to its rhythm, rocking my long-lost cousin.

The father entered and sat before the fire. The chanting stopped. The mother nodded her head at me and indicated a mat against the wall. She pointed until I went there and lay down. My arms kept Letty wrapped close against me. Eventually I was asleep.

Dreams came and went. Dreams of birds massing around me, pushing, squawking, flying into my hair, pulling my bonnet strings. I slept fitfully and wakened. Letty was still beside me, asleep. The fire had died down to red coals, giving an orange glow to the dark, domed walls. The family was all asleep around me; different breathing rhythms filled the night.

I shifted my position. It was still dark, although I had a sense daylight was not far away. *Now*, I told myself. *Now is the time to go. Leave this place, Tansy. You wanted to find Letty, and you have her. Just go!*

But where will I go? How will I raise a child? I knew not the answer to these questions, but the moment was ripe for action. I sat up quietly. Letty squirmed, took a loud breath. I froze, thinking she would awaken someone, but no one stirred. The blanket was wrapped around both Letty and me, and untwisting it made shuffling sounds. Still no one wakened. I stood and looked around. Silence. No one was moving. Quietly I crept outside.

My wagon was there, and oh, it was still filled with pigeons! No matter. Rufus brushed against me and licked my hand. "Oh, Rufus," I whispered. "Where is Maxwell? Find Maxwell, Rufus."

The moon was behind a cloud, and I could not see well in the darkness. *Behind the wigwam, Tansy. That's where the Indian father took Maxwell for water.* I tiptoed softly, but I bumped into something—or someone.

"Oh!" I cried out as I saw the glint of eyes before me. It was the Indian girl. She grabbed Letty out of my arms.

"No! No, you cannot have her." I pulled her back to myself. Letty awakened and began screaming. We tugged at her. First she was in my arms, then in the Indian girl's.

A cloud moved off the moon, and the silvery light revealed the terror in Letty's eyes. They were fixed on me, but she showed no recognition.

"Letty girl, it's Cousin Tansy." I reached for her again.

"Let her go!" I shrieked at the girl who held her tightly. "She is my child!"

A sharp word came from the mother, who, with the rest of the family, had come sleepily outside. The girl, looking angry, let go of Letty. I ran with her toward Maxwell, tied nearby, grabbed his halter with one hand, and rushed him toward the wagon.

"I go now!" I shouted. "Baby mine!"

The father, without speaking, took Maxwell's halter, and led him back behind the wigwam. I was left stunned and helpless, for I couldn't go anywhere without Maxwell. Gently, the mother took Letty, who was still crying, and retreated inside. The family followed her. I stood in the moonlight, alone, defeated.

Almost defeated, that is. For something happened to me in that moment, standing by the wagon with empty arms. As I went back over the happenings of the last few days, I realized that each time a barrier had been raised before me, it had renewed my resolve. Like the spider, who rebuilt her torn web, I *would* have Letty. I would! I would leave this place. With Letty. I just didn't know how or when.

* * *

CHAPTER 25

APRIL 1812

I nearly became an Indian. I was living with this family in their wigwam, eating, sleeping, helping, and caring for my cousin. No one treated me as an outsider now, although I was watched when I went very far away. The girl, especially, didn't trust me; she put herself between Letty and me sometimes, and made a clamor when I sang to my little girl.

When I would depart, I knew not, but I looked for every opportunity. I would know the right time. During the day I prepared food, ground corn, and fetched water. At night, before sleep came, I planned and re-planned.

This was a quiet family. No one said very much to me or to each other. The mother treated me kindly and was loving to Letty. The three little boys did nothing more than play with each other, eat, and sleep. Sometimes they went with their father into the forest to hunt, or to the fields to work the soil.

The Indian girl glared at me, or grabbed away my food, and even pinched me once. I understood her desire to keep Letty, for my own feelings for the child were strong. But she could not keep her. Letty did not belong here. She was not an Indian, even though the girl had put feathers and leather strings in Letty's hair. On warm days, Letty wore no clothing, just like the other small children in this village. I tried to dress her in clothes that I brought with me, but even the little frock Aunt Mary made for her was too small now.

Letty was beginning to be friendly toward me again, and my heart beat with joy when she smiled and ran into my arms. When I tickled her, I could make her laugh. When I sang my old, familiar songs, she seemed happy. The family looked at me strangely at those times.

We plucked pigeon feathers and ate birds every day. But they were beginning to taste bad and to smell bad, and I wouldn't eat them anymore. The corn and squash were adequate. I would dearly have liked coffee again, but that would come.

Rufus wouldn't eat pigeons anymore either. Enough was enough, for both of us!

Letty began coughing today, and she lay still on her mat, her cheeks bright red and warm, like she had the fever. No smiles, no giggles, no playing. The Indian mother gave her a drink with strong herbs in it, but she choked and spit it out, crying pitifully. I felt frightened, for I remembered Aunt Mary feeling poorly and each day getting worse until she died. Oh how I hoped Letty wouldn't get dangerously sick! The medicine man was summoned to come and heal her. At least I thought that's what I understood.

After three days, Letty was still feverish and coughing. I held her and sang to her, but she didn't rest well or seem to be improving. I took her outside to watch the boys in their play and to see Rufus, but she fussed and rubbed her eyes as if the light were too bright. Back inside the wigwam, she slept restlessly. When she wakened, she seemed listless and whimpered most of the day. The mother tried to get her to drink the potion again, but she would not swallow it. The Indian girl watched solemnly, saying nothing.

I held Letty on my lap as evening fell. Then she wanted the girl to hold her, then the mother, then me again. But she squirmed and cried when she was held or when lying on a mat. Her coughing went on and on. What was happening? Why wouldn't Letty get well?

Finally the medicine man came into the wigwam. He danced and chanted. His eyes pierced the night like flaming arrows, and Letty cried. He rattled some bones and touched Letty's throat, head, and stomach with them and sprinkled powder over her chest. Letty finally quieted and was soon asleep. I was relieved, for perhaps it meant she was better. We all had good, uninterrupted sleep for the first time in a few days.

In the morning, Letty was the first to waken. Her tossing about roused me. I noticed red spots on her face and neck. Looking more closely, I could see spots on her stomach, too. Measles!

The Indian mother sat up and saw me searching Letty's skin. She leaned closer, straining to see, then spoke loud, sharp words and began a mournful chant, rocking back and forth from one foot to the other. The children and father awakened. The father peered at Letty and quickly sent the children outside. "Go," he told them, and added some words I did not understand. Then to me he said, "Go! Leave village!"

How astonished I was at this turn of events!

"You send me away? Letty is sick!" I said. "Needs medicine!" I stood and wrung my hands. Was I to go alone, or did he mean for me to take Letty? Well, I certainly would not go without her!

"She needs care. And rest. Here!" My voice rose. "Medicine man come again." I looked to the mother, to the children for help. "Please," I pleaded. But no one spoke, or even looked at me.

"Go!" The father pointed toward the door. Then he went out.

I picked up Letty, blanket and all, gathered some possessions, and went outside. Maxwell was hitched to the wagon already, his ears drooping, shaking his head at a fly. Rufus saw me and jumped into the wagon. The three boys brought baskets of corn and beans, squashes, dried meat, and even two or three smoked pigeons, and dumped them in, next to Rufus. My provisions, including my rifle, were quickly added to the collection. Then the family stood back. Nothing was said. The Indian father folded his arms; the three boys folded theirs. A sense of impatience surrounded them. The mother looked at me without expression. However, I sensed a slight sympathy from her. The daughter, seemingly still angry, stared at me coldly. She was holding a long stick in her hand.

No one offered me assistance, so I started to climb into the wagon by myself. It was difficult, for I was carrying Letty. As I took the first high step, I pinned the blanket down with my foot, and I nearly dropped her. I couldn't move up or down. Still, no one came to help me. Finally I managed to get in. I pushed things aside, laid Letty down, then took the reins.

I had mixed feelings about leaving. My plans were not yet complete. I sat still and looked at the family. Where would I go? I didn't move.

The father said again, "Go!"

I jerked the reins. "Git, Maxwell. Git up." But he was still stubborn and wouldn't move. The father smacked him, and Maxwell took a few slow steps. At that moment, the girl rushed toward us and hit me on the shoulder with her stick. In a flash I snapped the reins again, and Maxwell began moving faster. I looked back and glared at the girl until she was out of sight.

Soon we were outside the village and heading into the forest. We plodded along for two or three hours. The sun had climbed to nearly straight above us, and the day was warming up. My thoughts flitted about like moths to lamplight, bumping into burning joys or zooming off into endless blackness. My only solace was knowing I had Letty with me. I looked at her. She was sleeping again. Measles were not usually too serious, I remembered. I was sure she would get well.

Maxwell retraced the path we'd taken. I hoped that meant he would get us back to the river. I didn't intend to go near Uncle Silas, however. We would avoid that part of the trail, even if I must go through tangled, thick brush. We would be back by the Mississippi in a day or two, and then . . . then?

Elder Jamison said I could get in touch with him, if need be. My mother and Corporal Dow had gone to Natchez. Maybe I could go live with them. One thing I wouldn't do was go back to New Madrid. Even though I could live in Uncle Silas's house, I knew he might return, and I refused to live that life again. It was over. Completely over. I had heard there were rich folks living in St. Charles. Maybe I could go there and be a housemaid; that is, if Letty could be with me. I wondered if it would be possible to find Mistress Wilson in that town?

I knew some folks had planned to move way out west, to be fur trappers. But I worried about Indians, who, perhaps, were warlike. Yet I remembered that Running Bear and Solomon had gone to live with the Osage. They were kind to white folks, it was said. Maybe I could find them, and . . .

Letty wakened and sat up. Poor little girl still covered with red spots. How pitiful she looked. I halted Maxwell. Time we ate something. I took out dried meat and fried bread. Letty and I nibbled on them. I tossed some hay to Maxwell; Rufus drooled on my shoulder until I gave him some scraps.

A breeze came up, carrying the pungency of the river in its breath. I must have been closer than I realized. A Carolina Parakeet fluttered from one tree to another, its brilliant green plumage flashing in the sunlight.

Letty smiled at me. "Tansy," she said, touching my cheek softly. A tingly thrill ran through me, welcoming the miles and days ahead. I smiled back at her.

* * *